Other Prowler Titles

Diary of a Hustler
ISBN 0-9524647-64

Young Cruisers
ISBN 0-9524647-72

Slaves
ISBN 0-9524647-99

Corporal in Charge
ISBN 0-95246478-0

Hard
ISBN 1-902644-01-8

The Young and The Hung
ISBN 1-902644-07-7

Aroused
ISBN 1-902644-08-5

Shipmates
ISBN 1-902644-14-X

Feeling Frisky
ISBN 1-902644-15-8

Paradise Palace
ISBN 1-902644-18-2

Virgin Sailors
ISBN 1-902644-03-4

Active Service
ISBN 1-902644-06-9

California Creamin'
ISBN 1-902644-04-2

Brad
ISBN 1-902644-09-3

Going Down
ISBN 1-902644-12-3

Summer Sweat
ISBN 1-902644-10-7

Riding the Big One
ISBN 1-902644-16-6

The Captain's Boy
ISBN 1-902644-23-9

The Initiation
ISBN 1-902644-17-4

the awakening ian cappell

prowler books

The Awakening by Ian Cappell

First printing February 2000. Printed in Finland by Werner Soderstrom Oy.
Cover photography by Glenn Studios © 2000 Millivres Prowler Group

web-site: prowler.co.uk
• ISBN 1-902644-30-1

British Library Cataloguing in Publication Data.
A catalogue record for this book is available from the British Library.

One

Steven had always been a normal, healthy, nondescript schoolboy. He was slim, with a mop of unruly light-brown hair and brown eyes. He played football, hated history, and was just as capable of getting into a fight in the playground as any of his peers. At thirteen he was hit by that terrible thing called puberty, and along with his mates he found a new pleasure in life, meeting them in the toilets at school, or in the changing-room after games. This was where they all, in various states of nervousness, opened their trousers, pulled them down, and exhibited their cocks for all to see, as they fisted them proudly, seeing who had the biggest! Who could shoot the furthest or the most of that strange white liquid that shot out of the piss-slit as they gasped and moaned and felt so good.

But this was seen, by all concerned, as nothing more than boys horsing around! It was something that boys did, nothing more. And besides, he thought it felt good to wank-off with the other boys and to see who could come the most. He soon learned that there were also a couple of boys in school who would suck cock too, if you let them! And, of course, if no-one else was around. But Steven was never interested in that. Even though it did cross his mind sometimes, when he was alone in his bedroom at night, lying naked with his solid cock in his hand for another wank before he went to sleep.

It wasn't until he left school and went to college just after his eighteenth birthday, that sex came knocking at his door for real. He was in the bedroom of one of his new friends, a boy called Mark, who was only three months older than himself. They had been drawn together somehow, right from the first day, and Mark's bedroom soon became the place where they most often worked together. The house was empty because Mark's parents were out for the evening, when suddenly Mark put down the book he was reading from, lay back on his bed, slid his hand down inside the front of his jeans and sighed, "I'm getting bored with this! I need to suck on a really hard cock and have some fun for a while!"

Steven looked shocked. Mark laughed as he stared at him, saying, "Don't tell me a sexy fucker like you hasn't had his cock sucked yet! Fuck me, Steven! Where have you been hiding all your life! It really feels great!" Steven then saw the large bulge in Mark's jeans as his friend was obviously stroking his hard cock. Mark went on, "Why don't you get those jeans open and I'll be glad to show you!" And before Steven could even open his mouth to speak, Mark not only pulled open the front of his jeans, but he slid them and his boxers straight down his smooth strong legs and took them right off, dropping them on the floor beside him. Then as he lay back, his solid seven inch cock and heavy balls on full display to his friend, he quickly unbuttoned the front of his shirt and spread it wide, so that Steven found himself staring at his friend's smooth, slender, naked body.

At once, Steven felt his own cock stiffening inside his jeans as he watched Mark stroking his solid cock while looking straight at him. Then he said, "Come on Steven! We're best friends aren't we? So what's wrong with us having a bit of fun together where no-one can see us!" Although he was very nervous, Steven had to admit that he had no argument against that! Especially as his own cock was by then really throbbing inside his jeans. Keeping his eyes fixed on Mark's sexy young body, his hands seemed to take on a life of their own, as they worked to undo the front of his jeans. He was sitting on the floor beside Mark's bed, and he got up onto his knees as he slid his jeans and shorts down his silken-soft thighs and his own rigid seven inch cock sprang into view. He stopped there, not quite knowing what to do next, but Mark encouraged him, saying, "Hey! That dick looks really delicious! Why don't you strip off completely like me, and we can really enjoy each other!"

Still feeling very nervous, and not daring to look Mark in the face, Steven undid the buttons on his shirt and slid it off over his shoulders, exposing his firm, well-developed chest and proud young nipples. Uncertainly dropping his shirt onto the floor beside him, he then set to work ridding himself of his jeans and shorts completely. Once he was fully naked, he was struck by the strange sense of freedom that wafted over him, and although he was still trembling with nerves, it seemed much easier to climb up onto the bed and lay down beside his best friend.

It only took Mark seconds to slide down the bed and, without another word he covered the head of Steven's cock with his warm wet mouth. The feeling was the most fantastic Steven had ever experienced, and he gasped and moaned as he felt Mark's tongue working on the sensitive head, then the warmth of Mark's lips sliding up and down on his solid throbbing shaft. Mark then worked his body around so that his cock was only inches away from Steven's mouth as he gave his full and undivided attention to giving his friend his first ever blow-job. Gazing at that throbbing cock, his body filled with the most delicious feelings he had ever known, it didn't take him long to come around to the idea that he secretly really wanted to do this too, and there, right in front of his face was the golden opportunity, waving around as if inviting him to just cover it with his mouth.

Glancing down his body he saw clearly just how much Mark was enjoying what he was doing, so, very sheepishly, and still trembling with nerves, he moved his head closer to that wonderful looking cock. And just as he felt Mark running his fingers through his wiry pubic bush, he covered the head with his mouth and felt the warmth and strength of it inside him. By then Mark was sucking on Steven's cock greedily, lapping, licking and slobbering over it, his hot young mouth was sending such waves of pure pleasure through Steven's body that it seemed to spur him on to return the wonderful favour his friend was doing for him.

Very soon he was thrusting his hips up and down on the bed, pounding his aching rod in and out of Mark's willing and eager mouth. As for the solid cock that was then inside his own mouth, he just instinctively knew, without any doubt at all, that he wanted it. Wanted to suck on it! Wanted to give Mark the same wonderful pleasure he was freely giving him. His nerves faded away, and he began to slide his mouth up and down on that beautiful hard shaft, slowly at first but soon getting into a much faster rhythm as he felt more and more natural about what he was doing.

It was then that he started to experience indescribable pleasure at having that love-pole sliding in and out of him. He couldn't take it all the way down his throat yet, not like Mark was doing with his, but he was determined that he was going to learn to, and the moans and groans escaping from Mark just served to make him want it all the more. By then they were both completely lost in what they were doing to each other. It was then, without even thinking about it, Steven slid his hands over as much of Mark's body as he could reach, and he heard him gasp even louder as his body seemed to tremble under this unexpected touch.

Automatically his fingers found and played with Mark's firm proud nipples, then slid smoothly over his young hips, finding and caressing his smooth firm arse-cheeks. Mark was moaning loudly around the cock filling his mouth, as he gyrated his body sexily under Steven's electric touch. All too soon for Steven's liking, he felt his cock swell in Mark's mouth and he knew that he was about to shoot. But instead of taking his cock out of his mouth, Mark just sucked on it all the harder, as he milked the hot creamy sperm out of him, making his head spin like crazy. This all felt so wonderful to him, that he didn't even notice Mark's cock also swelling in his own mouth, until suddenly it filled his mouth with its own hot, sweet, young cream. Again, it seemed perfectly natural to Steven to gulp this down greedily.

In fact, he felt very disappointed when it was all gone and Mark almost instantly slid his cock out of his mouth, got up off the bed and started to get dressed again. His friend had just awakened a strange and wonderful hunger inside him that he had never been aware of before. He not only quite naturally wanted to talk about it, he also wanted to do even more wonderful things with his best friend. But Mark seemed to behave as if nothing had ever happened, and Steven could see that he certainly was in no mood to discuss anything. In fact he seemed almost to be feeling guilty about what they had just done together, saying with his back to Steven, "I'm feeling tired! Why don't we call it a night, and I'll see you in college tomorrow." Silently Steven slid off the bed and quickly put on his clothes. Then he picked up his books and left, saying, "See you in class in the morning!"

But that certainly wasn't the last time they enjoyed sex together. Mark didn't mention it for over three weeks after that, and it was clear to Steven that he seemed to be having his own problems with it. But then it did happen again, and this time, it seemed that Mark was a lot more relaxed about it afterwards, when it really mattered. By then, both of them realised that they were different from the other boys. But each seemed to find a strange sort of comfort and security in the knowledge that they were not alone in their difference. They continued to enjoy their secret meetings for a whole year, during which time they not only sucked each other off, but they also explored each other's bodies with their hands, driving each other wild until they both shot their loads.

Their sex never went any further than that, by mutual, unspoken consent. It seemed that they were both completely content with what they shared together, and neither of them wanted to take things any further. Then one night, as they both lay naked on the bed, recovering from mind-blowing orgasms, Mark announced that he was leaving the college to move to another one up north. Steven was devastated and implored Mark not to go. But Mark informed him casually that it was all fixed, all the arrangements had been made already. And although he said that the move was because his new college had better tutors and better facilities, there was still a nagging doubt in the back of Steven's mind that his best friend suddenly wasn't being completely honest with him. Two days later Mark was gone. He didn't even say goodbye! Steven was completely devastated.

Two

Steven had been given a new bike by his parents, for his nineteenth birthday. He was very proud of it, and used to ride to and from college on it every day. After Mark left, he buried himself totally in his studies, not wanting to even think about Mark, or sex, ever again. He felt a strange emptiness deep inside, whenever he caught himself thinking about Mark. It was an emptiness that was very painful to him, and so he blocked these thoughts from his mind by studying really hard. However, he couldn't shut these thoughts out entirely, not at night when he was alone in bed, and his cock reared up to its full and aching hardness, forcing him to take it firmly in hand. Then he had no real choice but to lay there naked, fisting his cock harder and harder, faster and faster, as his thoughts took him back to those wonderful evenings in Mark's bedroom.

He would re-live all the wonderful feelings and sensations of being naked with Mark, as they sucked each other off and caressed each other's bodies so tenderly. Laying there with his left hand running all over his warm naked flesh, his mind completely lost to the touch of Mark's hands on his silken-soft skin. His right hand slid up and down the shaft of his solid aching cock harder and harder, his body heaving and covered in sweat, until after having delayed for as long as he could, he felt his balls pull up tight against the base of his cock. Then the wonderful heady rush, as the hot sperm coursed through his engorged shaft, and fired jet upon jet all over his heaving chest and stomach, as he gasped and panted for breath. While his cock was still pulsing madly, he would dip his fingers into the warm, pearly-white sperm repeatedly, and carry it to his hungry mouth, luxuriating in its taste and thickness, but imagining that it was Mark's sweet-tasting sperm, and not his own.

It was at these times that he had no other choice but to admit to himself just how much he really missed Mark. He also missed the sex they used to enjoy together, and this made him realise that he was missing not just sex, but Male sex! He knew of no-one else amongst his friends, or at college, that he could possibly do these wonderful things with. As for Mark, he was hundreds of miles away, and as Steven saw it, probably no longer wanted to do those things.

He still saw Mark occasionally in the street, when he was home on holiday or for a long weekend, and they would stop and talk to each other. But sex was never mentioned, and there seemed to be a kind of invisible barrier between them that had never been there before. Mark certainly never invited him to come around to his parents' house anymore, so Steven naturally assumed that he was no longer interested in doing anything with him, even though Steven still felt a wonderful stiffness inside his jeans, just from being near his friend.

One Friday evening, while he was cycling home, the chain on his bike came loose and fouled itself up in the gears. No matter how hard he tried he just couldn't free it, so after getting himself covered in oil and grease from the chain, he ended up having to carry his bike home. As soon as his father came home Steven told him what had happened, but try as he might, even his father couldn't release the chain. Washing his hands, he phoned the mechanic who serviced his car, and it was arranged that, as a favour to a good customer, Steven could take his bike around to his workshop the following morning. Steven was very down about his bike. It was very special to him, and he hoped desperately that Paul, the mechanic, would be able to put it right again.

The next morning, as arranged, he was up bright and early and made his way to where Paul had his garage-workshop. It was in an old part of the town, a lock-up garage under the arches of the railway track. The area was very run-down and seedy. Steven assumed that was the reason that Paul had his business there, because the rents would be a lot cheaper than in the better areas. It was sunny even then, and he was wearing a loose-fitting white T-shirt, a pair of old torn jeans and an old pair of trainers with no socks. He found the lock-up without to much trouble, and when he carried his bike inside, he found what he assumed was Paul laying on his back half under a car.

The lower half of the body, covered in dark-blue, grease smeared overalls, was obviously slim. He found his eyes locking almost immediately onto Paul's crotch as he lay stretched out before him, and instantly he began to wonder how big the cock might be that was concealed by those overalls. This thought surprised him a lot. He certainly didn't normally think about other young men in this way. He then became aware of the strong smell of grease and oil in the air, and strangely, to his complete amazement, it started to arouse him. He felt his cock stiffening fast inside his jeans. This in turn made him fix his concentration all the more on the crotch of the young body lying on the floor right in front of him. Suddenly, his bike completely forgotten, all that filled his mind was wanting to see what was inside those overalls.

The sight which met Steven's eyes, once Paul realised that there was someone standing near him, and pulled himself from under the car, was so wonderful that his cock throbbed madly and tented the front of his jeans so badly that even a blind man couldn't fail to notice it. Paul was young, twenty-one, with a slim face and jet-black, straight hair. He stopped dead, his face only inches from Steven's crotch, and tilting back his head, he gazed up the length of Steven's horny young body, smiling up at him. Despite his embarrassment, and the sweat breaking out all over his body, Steven just couldn't control his cock – it seemed to have taken on a life of its own. No matter how much he wanted it to go down, the damn thing just kept on throbbing, painfully hard inside his jeans, and he felt sure that at any moment the zip would just burst wide open under the pressure and his hard-on would slap Paul right in the face. As if Paul could read his mind, the smile on his face grew even broader as he gazed back down at the rampant bulge right before his eyes, then up into Steven's eyes as he said, "Hello! You must be Steven! I can see that it's not only your bike that needs some attention! Don't worry, I get the same problem sometimes!"

Paul then slowly got to his feet, and without any hesitation, lightly ran his fingers over the front of Steven's bulging jeans as he calmly slid his zip right down. This intimacy sent waves of pure desire flooding through Steven's body, making him gasp with pleasure as he stared, completely mesmerised, into the dark pools of Paul's eyes. It had been a very long time since Mark had excited him in this way, and now, there was something more, the smell of the oil and grease in his nostrils that on top of everything else was simply driving him wild, sending him totally out of control. This all worked on his senses, suddenly he saw nothing! Only this horny young man standing in front of him rubbing his solid throbbing cock with his hand. Already he was surrendering himself to whatever Paul wanted to do to him, and nothing else seemed to matter.

Seeing this, Paul reached inside the open fly of Steven's jeans and gently squeezed his aching hard-on, as he saw, with some satisfaction, Steven's lips part and his eyes begin to cloud under the rush of his desire. He let go of Steven's cock, and without a word, moved past him, walking over to the door, which he closed and bolted so that they wouldn't be disturbed. Then he went and stood by the workbench along the side wall, Steven's eyes following his every move.

Teasingly he leaned back against the bench, then very slowly, undid his overalls, slipping them a little at a time off his shoulders and down his arms. After a momentary pause, he watched Steven's chest rising and falling as his lust took absolute control of both his mind and his body. Then Paul continued to slide his overalls down the full length of his smooth, slender body, until he stepped out of them, standing there completely naked, revealing his own, now rampant, seven-and-a-half inch cock. Taking this in his right hand, he stroked the shaft fondly for a few minutes, all the time keeping his eyes on Steven and watching his unbridled lust almost ripping him apart.

Smiling at him sweetly, he said, "Is this what you wanted to see? Well now, why don't you get naked too, and we can both enjoy ourselves." Totally lost to his lust, with his painfully hard cock controlling his every thought, Steven almost ripped his T-shirt off over his head, then, as he kicked off his trainers he popped the button at his waist and slid his jeans and shorts down and took them right off, dumping them along with his T-shirt on the bonnet of the car behind him. Standing naked, with his throbbing cock in his hand; his mouth openly watering at the sight of the hot, naked young man before him, he didn't care what happened to him. The feelings and emotions that flooded through him were much stronger than they had been with Mark, and he knew that he wanted much more to happen with this young man, than just having his dick sucked. And strangely enough, he somehow already knew that he was going to get it.

The instant that Paul beckoned to him to come and stand in front of him, Steven was there. Standing with his body unashamedly heaving with lust, his mind in absolutely no doubt that whatever Paul wanted he would willingly submit to. His legs slightly apart, Steven allowed Paul to take his own hand off his cock and place it by his side. Then he moaned loudly as Paul began running his own hands over every inch of Steven's hot and trembling body. Just the touch of someone else's hands on his naked flesh made Steven so excited, that in only a matter of seconds of this delicious, wonderful torment, he became afraid that he would shoot his load right then and there.

Whenever he had been naked with Mark they had just sucked and caressed each other, but already he knew that this was something completely different. This was something brand new. Yes, he was afraid, but his lust was so powerful that he was completely under its control. No-one had ever stroked his arse-cheeks quite like this before, let alone spread them and run their fingers down his crack and brushed them lightly, teasingly across his virgin arse-hole. The feelings inside him were like a tingling electric current that was somehow setting him completely free. He had never felt this open before. Paul's hands were rough against his smooth, silken-soft skin, and the feel of them on his body was as if he was the clay in the hands of an expert potter.

Paul then turned his attention to Steven's nipples, rubbing his fingertips lightly over them making Steven's mouth open wide as he gasped at the wonderful sensations this sent wafting through him. And as Paul continued to do this, Steven heard himself moaning more and more as his head spun wildly. Then Paul was placing his hands on his shoulders, gently forcing him down onto his knees. Eagerly he took Paul's cock into his mouth and began sucking on it, while Paul gently caressed his hair and steered his head backwards and forwards on his cock, urging him to take it deeper and deeper all the time.

As he sucked on that wonderful hard cock, Steven smelled the oil on Paul's body as well as the sweat in his crotch. These two aromas coupled together just sent him wild. He sucked harder and deeper with every thrust of Paul's slender hips, and before he knew it, his throat had opened and Paul's throbbing cock was sliding smoothly all the way down his throat, so that his nose was being buried deep in Paul's bush of jet-black pubic hair and he was breathing in that heady man-scent, feeling his head spinning as his lust took full control.

All this time Paul was leaning back against the work-bench, thrusting his cock deeper and harder into his willing and hungry throat as he also moaned with pleasure, and encouraged Steven as he gasped, "Oh yeah! That's nice! You suck cock really well Steven! Suck it harder! Take it deeper! Yes! Oh yes! You must be the best fucking cocksucker I've ever had. Oooo yes! I can see were going to have some really hot fun together, you and me Steven. And that's no mistake."

But while Steven heard all this, he was already completely lost in his own little world of burning lust, a world that revolved solely around that fabulous hard cock sliding in and out of him as he fisted his own painfully hard cock frantically, looking forward eagerly to the hot, sweet load of sperm that he longed for, whenever Paul was ready to give it to him. Little did he know or care right at that moment that Paul had much more than just a naked blow-job in mind for his willing and horny young body.

On and on, Steven sucked and slurped on Paul's wonderful cock, loving the feel of it sliding in and out of his hungry young mouth. But just when he was fully expecting Paul to fill his mouth with his hot sweet load, he was suddenly startled when Paul grabbed him firmly by the hair, and pulled him roughly off the raging hard cock which he had been enjoying so much. For a split second he thought that he may have done something wrong, and the look of surprise on his face showed this very clearly. But in the same instant Paul pulled him roughly to his feet, wrapping his strong young arms around his body as he drew him close, so that they then stood, chest-to-chest, cock-to-cock, face-to-face. And before Steven had time to realise what was happening Paul kissed him full on the mouth and Steven felt his insistent tongue forcing his mouth open even wider.

At the same time, Paul's hands were once more exploring every inch of Steven's body, but much more firmly this time. Each stroke and caress driving him so wild with passion, he willingly surrendered and soon he was returning Paul's kisses feverishly, as his own hands explored Paul's body with the same determination; his mind swimming as he wondered what else this horny, and obviously experienced young man had in store for him. This was all so wonderful, so exciting, that he wished that it would never end. He felt Paul's muscular back, his firm, tight arse-cheeks and then, slipping a hand between their two sweating young bodies, he felt their two swollen and engorged cocks locked side-by-side between them. Steven was deliriously happy and entirely abandoned to his overwhelming lust.

But once again, just when Steven was starting to get used to all these beautiful new feelings and emotions, Paul broke their embrace and held him off at arm's length. "Well, my beautiful cocksucker! What else are you good at?" He asked with a broad grin on his face. Timidly Steven answered, "Nothing. All I've done before was to suck cock with my best friend at college. But then he went away to another college up north. But we never did anything like this! And I haven't been with anyone since then either."

Paul looked surprised as he lightly stroked Steven's cheek saying, "Well from the way you're turned-on, I think it's high time that you discovered all the other wonderful things that horny body was really made for, don't you?" Before Steven even had time to think, he heard himself reply, "I only thought I was coming here to get my bike fixed! I had no idea that after only about twenty minutes I'd be stark naked like this and feeling hornier than I have ever felt before! So you can do anything you want to me! Anything at all! Fuck me! Your body looks so fucking sexy!" Though right at that moment, he had no way of knowing just what he was agreeing too! He just felt so horny, so excited, that all he wanted right then was for those feelings and emotions to continue, and never end.

It was only then, that Paul noticed for the first time, that in his eagerness to get his hands on Steven's willing and eager body, he had completely forgotten to clean off all the grease and oil that his hands were covered in. But he then saw that Steven's clean body was smeared all over with streaks of oil and dirty grease. For him this was quite a turn-on, but he wondered if Steven was aware of this. "How do you like your nice clean body covered in dirty oil and grease?" he asked smiling broadly.

Steven looked down at his normally clean body, and at once he smelled the dirty oil that was now all over him. He sighed and breathed in the warm smell as he replied, "It feels really sexy! And the smell is turning me on something rotten!" Paul smiled even more. "Good! I'm glad about that, it's a turn-on for me too! I often plaster some grease all over my cock before I wrap my fist around it and start to pump off a load! It makes me feel really horny. How about we get you really plastered in it! Your body is much too clean for in here anyway!" They both laughed at this, and Steven stood still while Paul dipped his hands into a drum of dirty, smelly old engine oil that had come out of a car after an oil-change. This he plastered all over Steven's body, saying, "Don't worry! There's a shower over in the back there! So you can clean it all off before you leave!"

But Steven was already wrapped up in the smell and feel of it on his hot body. It felt fantastic, and his aching cock throbbed all the more painfully between his legs as Paul continued to smear it all over him. Then, once he was covered completely, Paul told him to do the same to him, something that Steven eagerly agreed to. Then they both held each other close, running their hands all over each others bodies as they breathed in the heady mixture of oil and sex.

Next Paul took a handful of heavy axle-grease from a large drum, and this he held under Steven's nose for him to smell before he wiped it all over Steven's rigid cock, his balls, and then turning him around, deep into his arse-crack. This new sensation was so electrifying that Steven thought he truly would shoot his load instantly. Taking him in his arms again, Paul kissed him more roughly, even more passionately. Only this time their bodies gyrated easily against one another because of the grease, and their two cock were gliding smoothly against each other as they both fondled and caressed, driving each other insane with lust. After doing this for some minutes, moaning and panting, Paul gently lowered Steven to the ground and laid him on his back on the dirty floor that was heavily ingrained with the dried oil and grease of many years.

With great care, he lowered himself on top of Steven's prone and eager young body, supporting himself on his arms so that he could work his body up and down the length of Steven's, brushing his rigid and painfully hard cock across his belly and chest, both of them lost completely in their burning lust for each other. After several more delirious minutes of this, accompanied by some tender kisses, Paul kept on doing it as he said, "Now for the best part, you sexy little fucker! How would you like my stiff cock inside your virgin arse? That will really make you feel good! Honest it will!"

He kissed Steven again, desperate with passion, then he continued, "In fact, you really are so fucking sexy, that I want to fuck your arse till your head explodes. I've had my fair share of man-sex since I started working here three years ago, with the old man who used to run this business. He was the one that first saw how the oil and grease affected my dick, after I'd only been working here a week! Then one afternoon, before I knew it, he'd locked the doors and just walked over to where I was working. He must have smeared some filthy oil on his hand as he came over to me, because the first I knew he held his hand over my nose and my head started to spin like crazy as my dick got as hard as iron! I just stood there in a trance as he opened my over-alls wide. I only used to wear my boxers under them back then, but he soon broke me of that idea, as I just stood there and he stripped me completely naked!

He did the same to me as I just did to you, he covered my body com-pletely in the shitty oil he'd just drained out of a car engine! The smell of that oil, and the feel of his rough hands running all over my naked body sent me as high as a fucking kite, I can tell you! All he did then, was bend me over the bonnet of a car, spread my legs wide apart while he slapped some axle-grease on my virgin arse, and worked it into my fuck-hole with his fingers. Before I knew it, I was getting fucked! His fantastic cock was all the way up me, he was slamming it in and out of me really hard, and I was wishing with all my heart that he'd just keep me like that forever! He fucked me four times that first afternoon, and made sure that my own cock got milked so much that my balls were dry by the time he'd finished with me!"

Paul sighed deeply, and his eyes were glazed with lust as he carried on rubbing his solid cock against Steven's slippery body. He went on, "While I was still out of my head with lust, and fucked stupid, he half-carried me into the shower and washed me as clean as you were when you first got here! By the time he had dried me off and put my boxers and overalls back on for me, I was coming down enough to be safe. So he told me to go home, and keep my mouth shut if I wanted to go on working for him!

The next morning when I came to work, he asked me how I was feeling! I just pulled open the front of my overalls, and showed him that the boxers had gone and I was naked under them, as I told him, I feel wonderful, sir! And as you can see, I'm ready to get fucked again anytime you want me! All you have to do is tell me to lock the doors, and I'll be out of these overalls before you can get your dick out! Fucking hell! I never needed sex from anybody else after that! Sometimes he'd even torment me by getting me to lock the doors and tell me to strip off my overalls. Then I'd stand in front of him, my cock already hard and aching, while he'd cover my horny body in dirty, stinking, wonderful oil! But instead of fucking my arse, he'd then make me carry on working, naked and as horny as fuck, my cock so painful it really hurt! But he'd keep me like that, no matter how crazy I was to get my arse fucked, until he was ready to take me!"

His cock slapped violently against Steven's belly while he was saying this, and Steven thought he was going to shoot his load. But he just carried on telling his story and driving Steven demented with lust at all he was hearing and feeling.

Paul said, "But he never once let me down, and before I went home at night, my arse was fucked so much it was gaping open, and my balls were drained completely! From then on, that used to happen most days. Then six months ago, he died! He left me this business in his will, and a note that just said, Keep up the good work, whenever you get the chance! Of course, because I'm young, there have been loads of customers or blokes just passing by the doors, that have come in and dropped their jeans for me! But I've never wanted to fuck someone, as much as I want to fuck you right now! Perhaps it's your kink for the oil and grease that makes me want you so badly! I don't know! But you'll really love it, having my greased-up cock sliding in and out of your arse! I promise you will! And if I've read you right, you'll not only love it, just like I did! But you'll want it up there again and again after that! Which means that you'll have to come back here often, and strip that beautiful, sexy body naked to get covered in this shit, and get your arse fucked long and hard, just like I used to! In fact, I'll make a deal with you! I haven't had a good shafting for over a week now! So if you let me fuck your virgin arse, and show you how good it feels, Ill bend over, and you can fuck your first arse too! How does that sound?"

Just for an instant Steven's fear returned, he had never thought of having a cock up his arse before, what if it hurt? Could he make Paul stop if he didn't like it? But Paul had already moved down his body and was kneeling between his open legs, lifting them up and folding them back towards his chest. He felt very vulnerable like that, then he watched as Paul reached for another dollop of grease from a tin near his head, and this he worked really gently over his virgin hole, then sliding first with one finger, then to Steven's wonder and amazement, two fingers all the way inside his arse. Yet weirdest of all was the fact that it didn't hurt a bit. Even Paul was surprised at just how easily his fingers slipped into Steven's hole and looked at him very puzzled as he said, "Are you sure you've never been fucked before?"

"No!" Steven assured him, "Why! Is something wrong? I promise you, no-one has ever done this to me before! I've never even thought about it before, let alone wanted anyone to do it to me! Not like I want you to, now! I don't understand why, but, the way I feel inside, you can do anything to me that you want to!" Paul smiled down at him and stroked his face saying, "No, my pretty virgin, there's nothing wrong. In fact I feel really good, that you want me to be the first, after I've told you how good it will make you feel inside."

He worked his fingers in and out of Steven's arse a few times, making the arse muscles relax all the more. Then he went on, "All this means is that your arse really is eager for it, that's all! You are a very special young man, Steven. Normally a virgin arse is really tight, and it has to be prepared very slowly to take a cock! But your arse is so hungry for my cock, that it has just sucked up two of my fingers as easy as pie. Now, hold your legs back against your chest for me, and lift your arse a bit higher, so I can line my cock-head up with it". Paul's confident manner had taken away the need for Steven to make a decision, and so he willingly did as he was told and lifted his arse up off the floor whilst at the same time holding his knees firmly against his chest.

Paul then placed his swollen cock-head against Steven's virgin rosebud, and sighed at the contact. Very gently he began to push forward. At the same time he told Steven to breath slowly, in and out through his mouth, because this would make the entry easier for him. Nevertheless, they were both still amazed at just how easily Steven's arse swallowed Paul's cock. Once the head was inside, the shaft just slid on in there as smooth as silk inside that warm, welcoming hole until his balls came to rest against Steven's smooth, firm, arse-cheeks.

All of Steven's fears were completely banished as he realised just how natural it felt, having the whole of Paul's throbbing, hard cock buried deep inside him. In fact it felt so good, that he wondered why he had never thought of asking Mark to do it to him. Both of them were feeling really good about the whole thing, as Paul smiled down at him and asked, "How does it feel to have your arse stuffed full with my cock?" Eagerly Steven answered, "It feels wonderful! Go on Paul, fuck my virgin arse! Fuck me hard! I want to feel every stroke of your beautiful cock inside me!" With encouragement like that, it was little wonder then that Paul gave full vent to his passion. Though in fairness, he did work up to his fucking pace slowly.

But seeing just how much Steven was really enjoying it, before long he was ramming his cock in and out of Steven's willing arse like an express train as both of them gasped and panted, the sweat pouring out of them. Lost in the wonder of his own lust, Steven even screamed out to Paul "Yes! Yes! Fuck me harder! Fuck my brains out! This is fabulous! Don't stop! Please, don't stop!" As he gasped for air and his body tingled all over, he became so carried away by all these incredible feelings, and as their bodies writhed and slid about in the filth on the garage floor, he rubbed his hands in it, then wiped them all over his chest, thighs, arse-cheeks, and even his face.

The smell of the oil was such an aphrodisiac to him, that he went totally wild, and he wanted that hot, rampant cock, to stay inside him for ever. Paul, and his beautiful, solid cock were all that mattered in the whole world to Steven, as he felt it sliding smoothly in and out of him, making his head spin with lust. Making him certain that he really would be coming back here often, to feel a lot more of the same. Suddenly Paul stopped and pulled his cock all the way out of Steven's arse. But before Steven could ask what was wrong, Paul told him to get up, and lay across the bonnet of the car on his stomach.

Eagerly Steven got up and laid his hot, sweating young body stretched out on the cold metal, spreading his legs as wide as he could, so that Paul could get right back inside him again. He was not disappointed. No sooner had his incredibly horny young body touched the metal, than Paul was between his legs again, ramming his cock back inside this willing young fuckhole as if he had never taken it out. And once again Steven was in ecstasy. He was being introduced to feelings and emotions that he had never known existed before. And he found that he truly did love everything that was happening to him. He was also quite certain that he loved Paul too.

While Paul kept up his relentless fucking pace, he reached forward and took hold of Steven by the hips, pulling him back onto his cock with every forward thrust of his supple young hips. Not only did this allow him to thrust even deeper, into what by then was no longer a virgin arse, but it also enabled him to reach around Steven, and grab hold of his grease-coated, and fiercely aching cock. This he then fisted furiously in time with his fucking. On and on they went until finally Paul felt the sperm churning inside his balls and he knew that his climax was near. Then he pulled right out of Steven's arse, and told Steven to quickly get down on his knees facing him.

Instantly Steven slipped to the floor, then leaned back against the wing of the car with his mouth open wide as he watched Paul standing over him, pumping his engorged for all he was worth. At the same time Steven fisted his own super-rigid cock dementedly, both of them lost in the heights of their filthy passion. All at once, Steven let out a loud gasp, as his cock jerked violently in his hand and sent wad after wad of hot white sperm shooting out all over his chest and stomach. Only an instant later, Paul's cock also began firing off the fullest load of hot sperm Steven had ever seen before; the first spurts cascading through the air, some even landing in Steven's wide open mouth. The rest went all over his face, and even in his hair. Both of them felt not only that their lungs were going to burst, but also felt as one with each other. And for Steven it was all so unspeakably wonderful, he was in heaven.

Three

Now that he had been introduced to real man-sex, Steven was eager to repeat the experience, and as often as he possibly could. Therefore, he was very happy that Paul was more than willing to agree to this, and the two of them were soon having regular sessions together, at least three times a week. Paul never turned him away, even if he arrived at the garage when they had not arranged to see each other. Just one look at Steven's horny young body standing there, and Paul would immediately close and lock the garage doors. Then standing by his work-bench, he'd strip out of his overalls and stand there naked, ready for some hot horny action, as he stroked his rapidly hardening cock, driving Steven insane with desire. Steven would then rapidly shed his clothes too.

Often this meant that Paul had to work many extra hours on the cars, to keep up with his workload. But he left Steven in absolutely no doubt at all, that his hot and horny body was well worth the extra work he'd have to put in. And sometimes, even after they'd enjoyed really mind-blowing sex together, instead of Steven taking a shower to clean himself up, then putting his clothes back on and leaving, Paul would ask, "If you have the time, how about we both stay naked, and you can help me get this car ready for the morning. It'll be a great help to me if you will. And besides, with both of us naked, and covered in oil already, we might want to have another session when we've finished the work!" He stroked Steven's arse-cheek sexily and kissed him. Then he added softly, "Or even before we finish."

Steven certainly never refused these invitations, and the two of them soon found that they made a pretty good team. Over the next twelve months they fucked together as often as possible, while enjoying their mutual kink. They worked naked, side-by-side, and both freely and openly explored their lust for each other to it's fullest extent.

In Steven's eyes, his life was complete. During the day he went to college and studied hard, although even there his cock was never less than semi-hard. In fact, it would only take the mere thought of Paul's naked, oil-smeared body to make it spring instantly erect, which he sometimes found quite embarrassing. But he didn't really care, he loved the feel of his hard cock inside his jeans, and most of all, he loved the idea of leaving college and racing around to see Paul in the late afternoon, knowing as soon as he got there, that Paul would lock the doors behind him, and they would spend another evening of naked lust together, which would make him feel even more fantastic!

He had tried fucking Paul that once, on their first meeting, and would sometimes do it when Paul really begged for it. Though he found that he didn't really like it half as much as having Paul's love-pole buried deep inside his own willing arse. But before they got into their kink, Steven also learned to lick Paul's sweaty arse out. Finding to his delight that when he buried the tip of his tongue as deep into the hole as he could, that this really turned Paul on. He also found that when he was licking or sucking Paul's balls that the smell of Paul's crotch really made his own cock throb and bounce around like mad.

But wonderful as all these things were, still the most arousing, mind-blowing thing of all for him was his kink for dirty oil and grease, and the good hard fucking that went with it. The second that his clothes were off and piled up on the clean newspaper Paul laid out on the work-bench, the two of them would work on each other's horny young bodies until they were both demented with lust. And when neither of them could wait any longer, Paul would plaster him from head to toe in the filthy oil and grease that he saved from the cars, before getting Steven to do the same to him. The smell and feel of it on his body never failed to drive him insane with lust, and he would feel his arse twitching like crazy as Paul fucked his brains out, until they were both exhausted and their balls were drained.

Paul also explained all about the massive turn-on he got from the smell and feel of the dirty oil and grease being plastered all over his sexy young body. He told him this was known as a 'kink'! And that it was something that some people found sexually arousing, whereas others didn't. Paul was certainly a good teacher, and Steven also came to understand, that there was nothing wrong with his having this kink. That there were many other men who liked, and were turned-on by the same sort of thing. As well as many other things like say, pissing themselves, or being pissed on, the smell and feel of leather, wearing skin-tight rubber suits. And many, many others, so he was not to feel that his particular kink was anything bad or disgusting! It was what turned him on, and that was all that mattered.

Steven was fucked in every position they could think of, and as well as loving every minute of it, he loved the fact that Paul kept coming up with new ideas for them to try out too. Like the time he tied him in the sling that hung from the hoist Paul normally used for lifting the engines out of cars. They had both had their normal first session, kissing, caressing, sucking each other, and were fully aroused. Then they plastered each other in the filthy, stinking oil that turned them on so much, when Paul announced, "Today I have a new surprise for you!" Steven's eyes lit up at this, as they always did when Paul showed him something new.

Taking Steven by the hand, he led him to the back of the garage, to where the hoist stood, suspended from a solid iron girder spanning the garage. There were two long chains hanging from a large hook, which itself was attached to the hoist by a chain-loop. Taking one of the chains in his hand, Paul ran it through his hands until he reached the eyelet in the end. This he then placed over the hook, then did the same with the second chain. Steven stood watching him in rapt fascination, wondering what he had in mind, as he stroked his rigid cock, watching every movement of Paul's wonderfully sexy body.

Opening out one of the chain-loops he had just made, Paul said, "I've been saving this one as a special treat, until you got used to our sexy games, just like the old man did with me! See that drawer in the left of the work-bench? Go and open it, and inside you'll four leather straps with clips on them. Bring all four of them here to me!" Steven quickly did as he'd been asked and was soon back holding the strange-looking straps in his hands. Letting go of the chain, Paul smiled, and slapped Steven on the arse playfully. Steven gasped, and his cock bounced up and down. Taking one of the straps, which Steven had seen had a kind of fur-lining, he wrapped it around Steven's left ankle and did up the straps to hold it firmly in place. He did the same to his right ankle too, and then used the other two straps on both of Steven's wrists.

This done, he walked over to the wall and unwound the smaller linked chain that ran up and into the hoist. Feeding this chain through his hands, Steven watched the larger, heavier chain move down towards the floor. When Paul judged that the larger chain was low enough for what he wanted, he again wrapped the smaller one around a piece of angle-iron that was bolted into the wall, then came back to stand beside Steven. Crouching down he then opened out the chain-loops across the floor and told Steven to lay down on his stomach, with the first chain across his chest. Steven trembled as he half-realised what Paul was going to do to him. But somehow the idea really excited him, as did all the really sexy things that Paul did with his horny naked body.

Dropping quickly to the floor as instructed, Paul positioned the two chains where he wanted them, then had Steven hold his arms out wide, while he quickly attached the snap-clips on each wrist-cuff to the chain. Steven was then held fast, with his arms spread out wide from his body. Instantly he felt a rush of delicious lust surge through him and moaned loudly as he felt the ache in his cock trapped beneath him. Paul laughed. Then he slapped Steven's arse again, a bit harder than before, making Steven suck in his breath. Paul said, "So you really are a kinky fucker just like me!" Then taking hold of Steven's right ankle he stretched his leg out before attaching the clip on the ankle-cuff to the second chain, then quickly did the same with Steven's left ankle.

This left Steven in a full spread-eagle on the floor, and already he was moaning and sighing as with his face on one side he said, "Now I'm com-pletely at your mercy! Who taught you this one, you kinky sod!" Getting down behind him, Paul took hold of his own solid shaft and deliberately ran the head of his cock up and down Steven's arse-crack, which was then spread wide for him. This wonderful torture made Steven gasp and moan even more, as he begged, "Oh please Paul! Push it up me! Please don't torment me like this, please! You know how desperate I am for your fabulous cock!"

But Paul ignored this and carried on stroking his cock-head across Steven's puckered fuck-hole driving him insane with lust as he said, "The old man taught me this little trick! I didn't tell you this before, but he was a right perverted bastard, and no mistake! But he'd weighed me up right, from that first time when he stripped me naked! Just like I think I've got you weighed up right! But don't worry mate! Ill be a lot gentler with you, than that sadistic old bastard was with me, and that's a promise!" He slapped Steven's arse-cheeks again several times, hearing him gasp and sigh as the pain and heat filled his young arse. Then he rubbed the head of his cock across Steven's yearning fuck-hole once more, and Steven thought he was going out of his mind with lust as Paul said, "Yeah! The old cunt really used to treat me rough! Slapping me around, pinning me down while he got those cuffs on me! Then dragging me over here to the hoist and fastening me to the chains so I was complete-ly at his mercy!"

He slapped Steven's arse again, then got to his feet, walked over to the wall, and taking down the smaller chain he began pulling one end through the hoist, so that soon Steven felt the chains he was bound to lifting up and tak-ing him with them. In no time at all Steven found himself suspended right off the floor at waist height, by his wrists, ankles, the first chain that passed under his chest supporting his body, and the second that supported his legs.

Fastening the smaller chain off, Paul came back to stand beside his swaying body, running his hands all over him repeatedly, making him feel fan-tastic, then slapping his arse again hard with his hands, until Steven's arse was blazing with heat and he was begging him to hit him even harder. All the time, Paul kept telling Steven about the things the old man used to do to him, some of them sounding quite brutal. But behind it all, Steven couldn't mistake the note of love and respect in Paul's voice.

Standing right in front of him, Paul took hold of Steven's hair with his left hand, and pulled his head up, while with his right hand, he repeatedly wiped his rigid cock all over Steven's face, only occasionally letting it slip inside Steven's slobbering, drooling mouth for a second, then sliding it out again to continue wiping his face with it as he said, "That old bastard used to beat my arse raw! He'd twist my balls till I thought Id pass out with the pain! He even had a pair of crocodile clips that he used to fix on my hard tits! And all the while I was strung up just like you are Steven! And if I screamed too much, he'd just ram an old oily rag in my mouth to shut me up, while he filled my body with pain! But at the same time, he'd run his hands all over me, or even suck on my dick for a while, so I was getting a mix of pain and pleasure!"

Paul sighed deeply and Steven could tell just how much he really missed the old man. And from the sound of it, all the really painful and sadistic things he used to do to his young body. But which it was clear to Steven, Paul obviously loved so much. Sliding his cock back inside Steven's mouth again and letting him really suck on it, Paul went on, "After a while I couldn't tell pleasure from pain! That's when he used to fuck me! And do I mean fuck me! He used to hammer his cock into my arse so hard, my body would start swinging in the chains. Then he'd just stand there holding his dick and let the backwards and forwards sway of the chains carry my arse on and off his cock all the way!"

Pulling his cock out of Steven's gaping mouth, Paul then went round him and ducked under his body, coming up inside the V of Steven's spread legs. He pressed his cock-head against Steven's hole hearing him gasp as he said, "Now my kinky friend, it's your turn!" And he slapped Steven's arse really hard with both hands, then instantly drove his solid cock all the way inside him. Steven gasped at the speed of Paul's intrusion into his fuck-chute. His mind was racing wildly, as Paul began fucking his arse, while keeping up a steady rain of blows to both of his arse-cheeks. All too soon he felt the chains begin to sway under the force of Paul's fucking, and he began to see what Paul meant by the constant mixture of pain and pleasure, as his total vulnerability was brought crashing home to him.

In no time at all, Steven was gasping and panting, begging Paul not only to fuck him harder, but to slap his arse harder as well. That was when he felt Paul take hold of his hips and use them as handles to really make his body swing in the chains. At once he felt Paul's fabulous cock slide right out of his arse, then almost at once slide right back inside it again to his balls, and still the blows rained down on him making him keep his arse as tight as he could on that fantastic hard cock that was fucking his brains out. Steven really was experiencing a completely new high at Paul's expert hands. But just when he started to get used to this harsh treatment, Paul waited until Steven's arse backed right onto his cock, then he grabbed Steven's cock and balls around the base and twisted them quite viciously. Steven yelled with this new pain that flooded through him, but at that same time he very nearly passed out as he felt his hot sperm shooting along his shaft with more force and intensity than he had ever known before.

As Paul continued to manipulate his cock and balls making him stay hard and be ready for the next mind-blowing orgasm he yelled, "Fuck me! You kinky bastard! Fuck me till I can't walk straight! Oh Paul, you were right! Maybe I'm not ready for the heavy stuff like you were! But I fucking know that I love this! Just as you guessed I would! Give it to me! Give it to me harder! I Paul! I really love you!" In response, Paul stepped up the force and severity of his blows to Steven's arse, even using a long, heavy spanner he picked up off the floor instead of his hand, to really fill Steven's glowing arse-cheeks with the delicious pain he missed so much himself. Then with his cock aching for release, he went back to fucking Steven again, thrusting deep inside him as the sweat poured out of them both, until he could hold back no longer and he fired his pent-up load of hot sperm right up inside Steven's well-fucked arse. Something that also triggered Steven to fire off his second load at the same time.

All of this had awakened in Paul the burning lust that he'd been forced to suppress since the death of his benefactor. And instead of keeping Steven in the make-shift sling as he himself had been kept, helpless and vulnerable, often for many long and wonderfully painful hours at a time, he lowered the hoist and released Steven from his bondage. But that certainly wasn't the end of their kinky session, not by a long way.

Laying on the floor with a panting and exhausted Steven in his arms, he kissed him desperately. Instantly Steven felt Paul's still-solid cock pressing into his body, as Paul moaned softly, "Oh Steven! Perhaps putting you in the sling wasn't such a good idea after all! I hope I didn't hurt you too much!" Steven kissed him again and assured him that he'd thought the whole thing was really neat! Then Paul went on, "I'm really glad! But now it's all fresh in my mind again, there's a burning ache inside me that won't give up till I'm back in that sling again myself, and someone is really battering and abusing my body much worse than anything I've just done to you Steven! If you really do love me, will you chain me up and give me all the wonderful pain and torture that I know I really need! You may not like some of the things I beg you to do to me! But you're the only one I could ever trust to admit all this to! And you're definitely the only one, I would ever dream of asking to do it to me. Will you Steven? Please?"

So strong was his love for Paul, and so strong was the yearning he could actually feel inside his wonderful sexy friend for what he knew he really needed, that Steven found he had no choice but to agree. Quickly, almost feverishly, Paul's fingers worked to release Steven from the wrist and ankle-cuffs and attach them to his own limbs. Then he got into position on the chains and while begging Steven to be as rough with him as he could, he offered only a token resistance as Steven secured his wrists and ankles to the chains. Once held fast, Paul then told Steven how to operate the hoist and soon he was suspended high off the ground, his entire body completely vulnerable to whatever Steven wanted to do to him. He even told Steven to go to the back of the garage and look right behind the shower, where he found a well-made wooden box, which looked as if it had sat there for many years.

Opening the box, Steven found inside all manner of things which even to his inexperienced eye he recognised as being really vicious implements of torture. Carefully carrying these back to where Paul was hanging in the sling, he wasn't at all sure if, when the time came, he would actually be able to use them.

But as he already knew, Paul could be very persuasive when he wanted to be. How else had he taken complete control of him and shown him all the wonderfully kinky things that they now enjoyed doing to each other. So it was that with a combination of Paul's earnest begging and pleading, along with the genuine need he could clearly both see and feel in his lover, that Paul got him to use every last one of those implements on his horny young body.

Paul kept Steven fully aroused by begging him to fuck his mouth or even his arse which he already knew Steven didn't enjoy so much. Just so that he could keep Steven's cock hard and so keep him turned-on and into all that he was doing. The levels of pain and torture that Paul lovingly endured that night, would at any other time have turned Steven's stomach. He did it because he truly loved Paul. And he saw that the need in him was so strong, so demanding, that in his own highly aroused and emotional state he just couldn't say no.

That session and subsequent ones, that happened occasionally afterwards, lasted late into the night. And by the time Steven finally released Paul from his bondage he couldn't even stand up he was in so much pain. But the smile of ecstasy on his lust-demented face reassured Steven that his friend was more than satisfied. And Paul made Steven go and take his shower, leaving him lying on the floor in delirious agony, then stand over him while he crawled painfully on his belly across the oily floor, into a corner where he covered himself with some filthy old sacking, just as the old man used to make him do, and fell asleep instantly, having warned Steven in advance, not to feel any sympathy for him, not to touch him or help him in any way, but to then put his clothes on, let himself out, and post the keys back through the slit that served as a letter-box and go home with his thanks.

All-in-all, Steven became used to being around Paul, and enjoyed their regular hot and horny sex sessions together. And as time passed, he felt so completely a part of Paul's life, that as far as he could see, there was no reason why things couldn't just continue as they were between them forever. So much so that it came as quite a shock to him, when after one of their really long and hard sessions using the sling, Steven came out of the shower and watched Paul crawl across the floor into his corner as usual. Then after he'd dragged the filthy sacking over him, Paul called him over. Kneeling down beside his friend and lover, Paul then announced quite calmly, that he wouldn't be able to see him for the next two weeks, as his wife was having their first baby.

Steven was struck dumb! He didn't know what to say, what to think. Until then, Paul had never said a word about his being married! Steven had automatically assumed that, like himself, Paul was attracted to other young men. It had certainly never occurred to him, that married men, and certainly not young, horny ones like Paul should want to have male sex as well. Not knowing what to say, he simply agreed not to come to the garage for the next two weeks. Then he quickly dried himself off, put on his clothes and left.

But as he cycled home that night, he felt really heavy, even depressed, even rejected, as well as confused and let down. Naturally, he had always thought that he and Paul were completely honest with each other. He had certainly never held anything back from Paul, so he couldn't understand why Paul hadn't told him about this in the beginning.

With his new-found hunger for sex in overdrive, to Steven, two whole weeks without his rampant sex sessions with Paul seemed like forever. Every night, in the safety of his bedroom, he would hurriedly strip naked, lay on his bed, and fist his aching cock furiously, thinking back on their long, hot sessions together and longing for the day when he could once more go to the garage and have Paul's fantastic cock back inside him again. Though with his new knowledge that Paul was married, he did find that his mental images of their horny passion together tended to lose some of their overpowering impact. And although his nightly ritual of servicing himself with his right hand did momentarily relieve his frustration, it was no longer a satisfying substitute for the real sex he had come to love and crave for.

He would feel his body all over and imagine that it was Paul's hands running over his heaving young body, not his own. Paul had taught him to really love his body, and his rampant sex-drive, and this enforced separation from the object of his desire, felt more like a cruel and unjust punishment to him. Yet all the time, he had to constantly remind himself, that he had done nothing wrong!

Mercifully time does pass, even when you're young. So finally the day arrived that marked the end of Steven's two weeks of solitude. It was a Friday, and Paul had promised him a really long and kinky session, that probably would last late into the night, to make up for his not being able to see him. Despite the fact that he now knew that Paul was married, and a father, he still looked upon him as his lover and the best-ever friend he'd had in his life! That day in college was a real nightmare for him. He certainly couldn't keep his mind on any of his classes. And try as he might, he just couldn't get his cock to go down, which meant that he spent the majority of the day trying his best to hide a rigid and throbbing erection.

His only thought that day was seeing Paul that afternoon, just as fast as his bike could carry him there. There was no question in his young mind therefore, that once inside the garage, he wouldn't be able to get out of his clothes fast enough. The instant he got out of college, he got on his bike and raced through the streets, almost colliding with several cars in his haste to get to Paul again. By bike the journey only took twenty minutes, but to Steven it seemed to take hours. Finally, his heart pounding in his chest, he slammed on his brakes and skidded to a halt right outside the garage doors. But instead of the big old doors standing wide open as normal, it suddenly dawned on him that they were locked and the place was in darkness. Then his heart hit the floor as his eyes took in the large sign that was fixed across the doors. It read simply, coldly:

TO LET
Lock-up garage with power supply.
Also existing auto-repair business.
Phone 748934.

His mind in complete turmoil, Steven was suddenly bombarded with all manner of thoughts; What's happening? Where's Paul? Why isn't he here, waiting for me like he promised he'd be? Why has he done this? Is it my fault? Have I done something wrong, that's made him go away like this? What am I going to do now? What about me! These thoughts flooded his brain until everything just became a blur, and he felt the warm tears streaming down his cheeks. He just stood where he was for several minutes. He couldn't move. Didn't want to move. As the tears flooded out of him, he felt so empty, so betrayed.

Suddenly he was half-conscious that he was riding his bike. He had no idea where he was going, nor did he care. His entire world had just crashed around him and all he was painfully aware of, was feeling completely empty and alone. Aimlessly he rode through the streets for several hours. But all he could think about was the horrendous pain that was ripping him apart.

Some time later, he found himself entering a wood that stood right on the outskirts of the town. He only vaguely remembered Paul saying something about this being where men went, late at night, to meet other men to have sex with them in the open air.

It was only then that he became aware of the fact that it was raining, and must have been for some time, because his T-shirt and jeans were soaked through and hanging heavily on his body. But he didn't care anymore, nothing mattered at all, now that Paul was gone and it felt as if his life was over. Getting off his bike, he stumbled through the mud and fallen leaves, as he went deeper and deeper into the wood. When he came to a fallen tree-trunk, he leaned his bike against it and then slumped down heavily, only half conscious of pulling his dripping-wet T-shirt off over his head, then dropping it on the tree-trunk beside him where it laid completely forgotten as he just let the rain that dropped from the leaves above his head spatter onto his back.

It was really strange. In his utterly confused state, the rain felt really good to him. It felt clean, almost as if it could wash away all this pain, confusion and misery inside. Not even aware that he was doing it, Steven idly began running his left hand over his chest and stomach, as if he really was washing himself. Instantly his mind shot back to Paul, and how they used to wash each other in the shower after their delicious sex sessions. Immediately his cock stiffened inside his wet jeans, and with his mind once again back in the garage, automatically his right hand undid them, reached inside and released his solid erection, which he stroked absently.

After a few minutes with the light fading, he became aware of the dark shape of a man standing directly in front of him. He had no idea how long the man had been there, of how young or old he was, nor did he care in his abject depression. The man was only a dark outline amidst the darkness of the woods, but somewhere in his confused mind, Steven guessed that from his build, the man was probably about thirty. Staring through tear-filled eyes, he could just make out that the man was wearing what must have been a black leather jacket, and denim jeans. It was only then, as he stared at the man more closely, that he realised the man had the front of his jeans wide open, and he was holding his solid cock in his right hand, stroking it slowly.

Without any thought for his surroundings, Steven moved his head forward and took the mans solid cock deep into his throat and then sucked on it with such expertise that the man was soon moaning with pleasure. As he did this, half his mind was with Paul. The other half just didn't care where he was. There was a rigid cock in his mouth, and nose quickly filled with the heady man-scent from the stranger's groin. Suddenly, nothing else mattered.

He had been sucking the man's cock for about five minutes while pumping his own with his right hand, before all at once, it was pulled from his mouth. Then, in his dazed state he offered no resistance and allowed himself to be lifted to his feet. He stood there silently, only half-aware of what was happening to him, while the man stripped him completely. The man was quite rough in his handling of him, but Steven didn't care. He was then roughly pushed down onto his hands and knees in the mud and rotting leaves. Then his arms were kicked away so that he fell forward, his face and shoulders buried in the deep mud, while his arse was high in the air. Only then did the stranger speak, as in a gruff voice he sneered, "That's right, you dirty little cock- sucker! Get your filthy young body down in the mud where you belong, and spread those legs good and wide! My hard cocks going to fuck the shit out of you! Come on, get those fucking legs wider!"

Without even thinking, Steven did exactly as he was told. Soon he felt some grease being slapped on his exposed fuck-hole, followed almost immediately by the mans solid cock, which he rammed all the way into him without stopping. The force of the entry made Steven feel as if his entire body was being pushed into the ground. But the man showed no concern for him at all, and just started fucking him viciously.

It hurt like hell being taken in this way, as well as being utterly humiliating, having most of his body pushed backwards and forwards in the squelchy mud by the sheer force of the cock hammering in and out of his arse. He struggled a couple of times to raise himself up on his arms. But each time, the man just barked at him, "Get back down there where you belong, fuck-hole!" So Steven remained where he was, aware of only one thing, the wave upon wave of tremendous and overpowering lust and desire that flooded through his body, as his own swollen cock was being massaged by the mud beneath him. His lust for this abuse soon had him calling out, "Fuck me harder Mister! I love your cock inside me, it's what I deserve! Fill my cock-sucker's arse with your hot man-sperm! Plaster me with mud Mister, I want to be your dirty little fuck-boy! Please, fuck me harder! Harder! Please Mister! Oh I really need it bad!"

All this dirty talk quickly had its effect on the man as he scooped up handfuls of mud and plastered Steven's back and arse with it, all the time fucking him harder and more viciously. But Steven only moaned into the mud in his ecstasy, until finally, with one last surge of energy, the man lunged deep into his arse and let go his hot load. At the same time, Steven gasped as he felt his own hot sperm oozing from his cock beneath him, to mix immediately with the cold, churned-up mud.

But no sooner had the man finished shooting his load, than he pulled his cock out of Steven's arse. Feeling exhausted, Steven slumped down in the mud, and in seconds he heard the sound of the man walking away. Strangely he didn't care. Somehow, this anonymous sex had made him realise that there really was life after Paul, even though the squelchy mud that he lay in, only served to remind him of the oil and grease of the garage.

Only a few minutes later, Steven heard someone else coming up behind him. He lay perfectly still in the mud, and in seconds he felt two strong hands taking hold of his hips, lifting him up onto his knees. He moaned and spread his legs wide, and within seconds a new hard cock was sliding smoothly all the way inside his well-fucked arse. The newcomer fucked him with the same vicious urgency as the first, and soon he felt a second load of hot sperm filling his gut. Then the cock slid out of him and he heard the man walking away. It was then that he realised that throughout the whole thing, not a single word had been spoken. But neither did it seem to matter either. After all, why did he need to have feelings for someone to get his arse fucked?

His cock raging hard again from the last fuck, he felt it pulsing deliciously beneath him. Slowly he worked his body up and down in the mud, moaning and sighing as he felt all the wonderful sensations this sent rushing through him. While in his mind he lay there and waited for the next hard cock to fuck him wild. He stayed like that for what seemed like ages. Luxuriating in the feel on the oozing mud on his cock, and the sperm slowly sliding out of his well-fucked arse. But when no-one else came to slip their solid cock up inside him, he had only just risen to his knees, intending to take his wonderfully aching cock in hand as he knelt in the mud and really pump it hard, until he shot his load, when out of the corner of his eye, he realised that there in the darkness was another figure, standing just the other side of the tree-trunk, and looking down at him.

From the outline he thought this person to be much younger than the men that had fucked him already, maybe even his own age. Then Steven noticed that this young man also had his jeans wide open, and was stroking his solid cock with his right hand as his left hand seemed to be playing with his balls. Immediately Steven fell face-down in the mud and spread his arms out on either side of him. At the same time, he spread his mud-covered legs wide and pushed his arse up as high in the air as he could.

Feeling his rigid cock driving him insane with lust he called out in a clear voice, "My holes open house tonight, if you want to slip inside it. If you watched the other two men that have already fucked me, you'll know that you won't need any grease. Just plough on up there and fuck the shit out of me! I'm just a kinky fucker, who can't get enough of a good thing!" But nothing happened. He waited for a few minutes, and when still nothing happened his first thought was that the young man must have walked off and he hadn't heard him go. When he finally got to his knees again, Steven was surprised to see that the young man was in fact still standing there. Except that he had silently stepped over the tree-trunk so Steven could then see that he had already shot his load, though he was still holding his cock in his hand, and the thick white spunk was running over his fingers.

Steven guessed then that he must be just a watcher. Paul had told him that sometimes boys like him, in their late teens would come out here and just stand and watch other men having sex, while they fisted their own cocks. But that they were usually too scared to do anything themselves. Suddenly the stranger spoke, and Steven froze on the spot as his mind reeled in recognition. "Well Steven, you kinky fucker, I see you've come a long way since we used to suck each other off in my bedroom! I've been watching all the time, and as I watched those two men fucking you, and realised that it really was you, your arse looked so inviting that I very nearly did slip inside it myself".

Steven scrambled to his feet, to stand unashamedly naked, his rigid cock sticking out before him, and his body covered in mud before the stranger. It was only then that he realised that the rain had stopped and that the moonlight was filtering through the trees. It was by this half-light, that he was finally able to see the face that belonged to the voice, and in that instant his broken heart jumped for joy. "Mark!" he exclaimed, "Is it really you? And are you really still the same as me? WOW!" "Yes Steven! I'm still the same, and just as randy! The only reason why I left to go up north was because I felt then that it was wrong. That getting away from you, it would give us both a chance to sort our heads out. And the reason why I've never said anything to you when we've met in the street, was because although I soon discovered that for me this wasn't something that was just going to go away. I was afraid that you might feel the same anymore. So instead, I used to go home after seeing you, go and shut myself away in my bedroom, strip off my clothes, and have a fucking good hand-job just thinking about you. If only Id known you still felt the same way too, we could have been fucking like rabbits all this time!"

Mark realised then that his fingers were still covered in sperm, so he brought his hand to his mouth and licked each finger clean in turn as he said, "Come with me, there's a stream over there where you can clean up, then we can go back to my place. I live on my own now, ever since my dad walked in and caught me in bed with another young bloke I met one weekend. Actually, I was right up him at the time, and my dad was not too happy about it, so, he kicked me out and told me never to come back! I could have found a flat near the college I suppose, but for some strange reason I still wanted to have a place here that I could come back to! My gran left me some money in her will, so there's no problem paying the rent or anything. The bank does it all for me anyway!"

Mark then carried Steven's clothes for him, and wheeled his bike over to the stream, where Steven hurriedly washed off the worst of the mud. After wringing out his T-shirt, he used this to dry himself with. But just as he was about to put it on and then reach for his jeans, Mark snatched it from his hands and quickly draped it over the cross-bar of his bike along with his jeans. Then he took Steven in his arms and kissed him, long and passionately, while running his hands all over his beautiful, naked body.

Steven felt the painfully aching in his rigid cock as his passion soared. Feverishly his fingers worked to get Marks shirt open and his jeans and briefs down around his ankles so that he could look at, and touch, the body that had started him off on this kaleidoscope of lust and insane passion. Tenderly he covered Marks proud left nipple with his warm wet mouth and sucked on it just as Paul had taught him. Mark gasped with delight as Steven showed him yet something else that he had learned in his absence. With Mark taking the lead, they then took turns in sucking on each others rampant cocks and licking each other's balls. But when the moment came when Mark tried to bend Steven over to stick his rigid cock up his arse, Steven suddenly stopped him saying, "No Mark! Please, not here! Lets wait until we get to your place. We've got a lot of catching up to do! And besides, I did something here tonight, that

I would never have dreamed of doing, just letting those two men fuck me like that!"

He smiled at Mark weakly, then he went on, "I suppose Ill have to tell you all about that too. So take me back and show me your flat. And I promise, then you can have my arse all night, if you want it!" A little reluctantly, Mark stood back, and let Steven get his clothes on, while he buttoned up his shirt, pulled up his jeans and briefs, and stuffed his rigid cock inside them, having no small difficulty in then fastening them up. Then when they were both ready, Steven wheeled his bike, and the two of them left the wood side by side.

Four

Marks place turned out to be a single attic-room at the top of the house, right under the eaves. As they walked in through the door, the first thing that Steven saw was an old double bed with a big wooden headboard, in the left-hand corner of the room. This took up about a third of the floor space. Next to the bed was a window which looked out onto the street far below. To the right of the window stood a small kitchen table, with one straight-backed kitchen chair under it, and there were two wooden shelves fixed to the wall about three feet above the table. A small table-top electric cooker stood on a wooden cupboard next to the table, in the recess beside the chimney-breast. And in the opposite recess stood a kitchen-sink unit. There was an old-fashioned wardrobe with a mirror set into the door, standing against the wall next to the door, and two old and worn fire-side chairs, one on either side of the old electric fire, that stood in front of what had once been the fireplace. The wallpaper was hanging off the walls in some places, and in others it had already been stripped off. The landlord had told Mark that he would get in and decorate the room for him while he was away. But so far this had not been done. Nevertheless, to Mark this was now his home when he came back from college, the only home he had. And besides, he was never normally there for more than a week at the most.

But Steven saw the place through very different eyes. Although all the furniture looked really shabby and worn out, to him it seemed like a palace. Here, he could be alone with his Mark. Behind that door, just like in the garage, they had total privacy. Except that here there was no-one to tell him it was time to go home. His thoughts and dreams were interrupted, as Mark said, "You'd better get those clothes off and have a bath. There's a washing machine downstairs that we all use, and the bathrooms right next door".

Immediately Steven stripped off his wet, muddy clothes and gave them to Mark, who having checked that the coast was clear, then led a naked Steven out onto the landing and into the bathroom. While the bath was filling, Mark explained that he was very lucky in so far as there was no-one else living up here. This meant that he had the bathroom virtually to himself, and that the only time anyone else came up to use it, was when the other two bathrooms were both occupied. And that only ever happened rarely.

Mark left him, to run downstairs and put his wet, muddy clothes into the machine, but the instant he returned to his room, he too ripped off his clothes and silently slipped back into the bathroom, and got into the tub with Steven.

Although they both took turns at washing each other, naturally their cocks soon stiffened and their passion for each other soared. It was little wonder therefore, that they hardly bothered to stop and dry themselves before diving back into Marks room and getting their hot sexy bodies entwined on the bed.

In no time at all, Mark had Steven on his back with his legs folded against his chest, while he lustily drove his solid cock in and out of his friends arse. At the same time, Steven pumped his own rigid cock in his fist while staring up at Mark through glazed eyes, and thinking how lucky he was that he'd been in the woods that night to rescue him, fully aware that in the state of mind he was in then, anything at all could have happened to him.

Mark then pulled out of his arse and had Steven get up onto his hands and knees on the bed, then he slid back up him again and carried on fucking. Steven gasped and moaned as he shot his load into his hand, then carried the hot sperm to his mouth and licked it all off, as Mark continued to plough his cock deep inside his hungry fuck-hole. Finally Mark shot his load, burying his rampant cock all the way up Steven's arse and filling him with wonderful hot sperm, and the two of them collapsed onto the bed with Mark laying on Steven's back, their bodies both running with sweat.

Having renewed their intimacy with each others sexy young bodies, they lay for some time face-to-face, stroking and caressing each other tenderly, the after-glow of their passions bringing them together once more, making both of them realise that in some miraculous way, they had at last found the part of themselves that had been missing for a very long time. As they kissed and held each other close, so Steven told Mark truthfully all that had happened to him since that first day when he took his bike to be repaired. He left nothing out, though he could see that some of the things he was saying shocked Mark, especially the parts about when he was bound in the sling and Paul was beating his arse. But then, he wasn't at all ashamed of anything that he had done with Paul, neither was he ashamed of the fantastic feelings and emotions this kinky sex had awakened and aroused inside him.

Then he listened patiently while Mark told him about the young men he had fucked, though to Steven's ears, after all that he had experienced, it sounded pretty tame. Finally he asked, "Why do you think Paul just went away and left me like that? Its the one thing that I don't understand. And it still hurts, even now when I know I'm safe and wanted, here with you."

Mark was silent for a few seconds as he stared into Steven's eyes. He kissed him again tenderly, then brushed his cheek with his finger as he said, "There's no way that either of us can really know the answer to that question Steven. But from all that you've told me, it sounds as if that old man discovered that Paul really was a kinky bastard. Some men are, and the more pain and humiliation they get, the more they want. It becomes like a burning hunger deep inside them – almost like a drug. And although they can have normal sex, and enjoy it, for them, there's always something missing! So I suppose when the old man died like that, it must have hit Paul really hard. After all, who was he going to find that would understand his needs then. Not everybody can cope with that degree of kinkiness! I certainly don't think I could anyway!" He laughed. But seeing the seriousness on Steven's face he went on, "Like he told you, meeting you, and finding that you got turned-on by the smell and feel of filthy motor oil, brought it all back to him! And when he saw just how eager you were to go there and get your arse well and truly fucked, and share in his kink, I suppose it was only natural that as time passed, he'd then open up to you, and tell you all the things the old man used to do to him! In you he'd found someone that shared the same kink! Someone that would understand him, and not laugh in his face! Someone who would let him fully express the burning need inside him."

Steven's eyes were filled with wonder as he stared deeply into Marks and listened intently as he continued, "But it was probably that same freedom you gave him, that in the end scared the living crap out of him! Most likely he saw himself becoming more and more dependent on you, to be able to enjoy and have what he knew all along he really needed. Perhaps he realised that his kink was taking complete control of him again, as by the sound of it happened with the old man. So he got scared in case you just turned around one day and said you wouldn't be coming to see him anymore, because you'd found a boyfriend or something. Oh don't get me wrong Steven. I don't profess to be an expert on gay sexuality either. There are probably things locked deep inside me, that I haven't discovered yet. But perhaps I do know a little more than you do. And Id guess that something as powerful as that could very easily take over a person's life completely. And that's all right, if it's what you really want! I've certainly got nothing against it! As long as you have a stable partner, who recognises your need, and whose always going to be there to let you have it, and keep you safe. I certainly don't believe the story about him being married and his wife expecting their first baby! No way! I think he genuinely panicked! And his first thought would be to try and get his secret need back under control again.

He probably thought that the best way for him to do that, was for him to invent this story and distance himself from you, because you were the one person who was bringing this all out of him again. Then, as the days passed, perhaps he found that his hunger for heavy domination and brutality was just getting stronger, instead of fading away as he'd hoped it would. He probably panicked again. So he put the garage and the business up for sale and pissed off somewhere. In a way I feel very sorry for him!" He saw the puzzled look on Steven's face. Kissing him lightly on the lips, he went on, "Yes! I really do feel sorry for him. You see, either he probably thinks that by getting as far away from you as he can, hell be able to start again, in another town, and life will return to normal! Or he's decided in his own mind, that you wouldn't stay with him permanently, and that now his lust for brutality has got full control of him, he's got to somehow find someone, somewhere, that will stand by him, and treat him the way he needs to be treated, for the rest of his life! But sadly, my beautiful, wonderful Steven, whichever way he goes, hell never win. In fact, from all that you've told me about your own feelings in all this, Id say that he's probably run away from the one person in the world that not only did understand him, but who would have stood by him, if only he'd been prepared to trust you completely."

Steven sobbed, "I really did love him, Mark! With all my heart! I owe everything to him! He was the one taught me all about real man-sex! And made sure that I understood it was nothing to be ashamed of! He even taught me not to be ashamed of my own kink, for getting plastered in stinking motor oil, that turns me on something chronic! I'm sorry Mark, I probably shouldn't even be saying this to you! After all, I know now that I loved you in the beginning. And I do now! So please don't be angry with me! But if only Paul had told me the whole truth, Id have left home and left college, so I could live with him, and we could be together all the time. He could have worked naked, with the doors locked all the time. Id even have learned to enjoy fucking him, to make him happy. There was no need for him to just go off like that and leave me, without saying a word. Without even telling me how he really felt." He sobbed bitterly for several minutes while Mark just held him tight. Then he went on, "But though we can only guess at what really happened, what you said does make sense to me."

Raising his head from Mark's shoulder, Steven stared deeply into his eyes as he continued, "And now, I feel sorry for him too! He was so beautiful Mark! And I really did love him! I hope with all my heart that he does find someone who will understand him! And even if we never meet again, Ill always be grateful to him, for everything he did for me." Then he searched from one eye to the other repeatedly as he asked, "Can you understand that Mark, and still accept me, now you know I'm not the virgin you knew before? Can you?" Pulling his head back onto his shoulder Mark squeezed him tight, as he answered, "Yes, my beautiful Steven, I can. As long as you can forgive me, for running away from you the way that I did, in the first place." Then it was Steven's turn to squeeze Mark as he laughed saying, "Yes! Yes! YES!" And with love in their hearts they kissed tenderly, then held each other as they closed their eyes and drifted peacefully off to sleep.

The next morning Steven woke from a deep, dreamless sleep feeling a new and beautiful sensation as he lay there on his back. Opening his eyes he realised that Marks warm body was lying across his, under the duvet, and that it was Marks warm wet mouth sending all those wonderful feelings flooding through his body, as he gave him a morning blow-job! Steven had never felt so contented before, and he just lay there and enjoyed it, moaning softly as he felt Marks mouth working up and down on his solid shaft, until finally he rewarded his friend with his hot sweet load. But even though Steven was by then happily fingering Marks exposed arse-hole, which must have been turning him on something rotten, nevertheless Mark stayed under the covers, until he'd made sure that he had drained every last droplet of spunk from Steven's cock. Only then did he come up with a big grin on his face, and they kissed lovingly, wrapping their arms and legs around each another before Steven pushed Mark onto his back so that he could return the favour.

After that, Steven experienced something else completely new. That was for them both to remain naked in the privacy of their little haven, while they sat in the armchairs and enjoyed a leisurely breakfast together. Chatting happily as they ate, they talked about the events of the night before, out in the woods. Then more intimately, their feelings for each other. By then there was no doubt in either of their minds that they were both right for each other. In fact, they both agreed that living their separate lives, had brought them both nothing but pain, sadness and disappointment. So it was jointly decided, that Steven should leave home and move in. It was also decided by Mark, that as both of them wanted a full-time relationship, after being apart for so long, Mark would write and ask his principal for a transfer back to the same college as Steven. But as they both well knew, the chances of him getting it were pretty slim, he said that if he was refused, he'd drop out of college and get a job instead.

After breakfast, they then had another bath together, fighting hard to keep their lust for each other under control. They then got dressed and went together to Steven's home to talk to his mother about his leaving home. They were both very surprised when she readily agreed to Steven's moving out. Saying that it was good for boys their age to learn to look after themselves and make their own way in life. She also added to Steven while they were making coffee alone in the kitchen, that she had liked what she had seen of Mark, on the few occasions when Steven had brought him home for tea after college. And she was sure they would both get on very well together.

This made Steven feel really good inside. He loved his mother very much and it was very important to him to have her approval. Even though he had not told her that he and Mark were gay, and that they were actually lovers. Between them, they packed Steven's clothes, his hi-fi, portable TV and other things that he wanted to take with him. While they did this, his mother also sorted out some things to help them both set up their new home. It took several trips to move everything around to Marks room. But they worked happily together, and eventually Steven had moved in with all his possessions. They then spent the rest of the day unpacking and integrating Steven's things with Marks. They worked together cooking a nice dinner as part of their celebrations, sitting watching TV while they ate it.

Late that night, having washed the dishes and tidied the room up, they then enjoyed the most special time of all. Laying on the bed kissing and caressing each other, they gave free rein to their passions. Feeling their cocks hardening between their horny young bodies, they slowly stripped each other naked. And with the whole night ahead of them, they made love, slowly and passionately. Mark fucked Steven's beautiful, sexy arse in every position they could think of. Holding himself back until Steven was going crazy to have his hot sperm shoot inside his lust-filled body.

Needing time to regain his strength, Mark then turned his attention to Steven's rigid cock as well. Licking up and down the length of the throbbing shaft, sucking on his balls, driving him wild again, and making him suffer yet more wonderful torture, until Mark was ready to finally milk his balls of their sweet cream. Then Mark spread Steven's legs and fucked him again. Steven was delirious with this treatment by his lover. It went some way to giving him the same wonderful high that he had loved under Paul's sex-crazed control, and he loved Mark even more, for showing him this way that his body really was this desirable to him.

Afterwards they lay naked and exhausted in each others arms feeling totally relaxed and at one with each other, gazing around the room, which looked a lot more like a home with all their things in it. Both of them were sure in their hearts and minds, that whatever life may throw at them they would face it together and so be all the more capable of handling it. And with a final, tender kiss, they drifted peacefully into a blissful sleep, neither of them with a single care in the world.

They spent the whole of Sunday naked in their room, kissing, fondling, caressing each other, between making drinks and food, watching television; they even had sex in the bath. But on Monday morning, Steven washed and dressed, then went off to college with a real spring in his step, while Mark stayed at home and wrote the letter to his principal asking for the transfer, then he spent the day doing his own course-work for college. But he was outside Steven's college, waiting to greet his lover when he came out, and the two of them went shopping together to buy more food. Something that Steven had longed to do with Paul, but had never been allowed to. In fact, they soon settled into a regular routine, and for both of them, it quickly felt as if they had been together all of their lives.

Each morning they got up, and Mark made them both breakfast while Steven had a wash and got books and papers ready for college. After that, Steven got dressed; that was if Mark would let him. Sometimes, when Mark was feeling really horny, he would let Steven get his boxers or briefs on, and have his shirt half-buttoned up, then he'd get up and stand in front of Steven, gently pushing his hands away as he said, "Here! Let me do that for you!" Steven fell for it every time, because instead of doing up the buttons, Mark would immediately un-do them again. Then, as Steven looked at him in amazement, Mark would close his hot mouth around one of Steven's nipples and begin sucking on it hard.

Mark knew exactly how sensitive Steven's nipples were. He knew that once Steven felt that wonderful pain-pleasure that turned him on so easily, flooding through his body, his cock would harden instantly, and in seconds his shirt and briefs would be off again and he would be laying on his back on the bed, with Mark right on top of him. It wasn't unusual for Steven to be late for college. But he didn't mind this, and took the rebukes he received from his tutors, knowing full well that with Mark, he was powerless to ever say 'no' when his lover wanted his body. He just made him feel so horny, so wanted all the time.

Sadly, though not unexpectedly, Mark's request for a transfer was denied. But he certainly wasn't phased by this. Instead, he met Steven from college one day with a broad grin on his face as he announced, "I've got a job! I just went for an interview at Marriots! The personnel manager was really nice. I start on Monday morning, working in the offices!" Steven's eyes were wide with excitement, and only just stopping himself from kissing Mark, threw his arms around him and they hugged each other instead. Then they walked home together.

But the instant they got home and their door was closed behind them, Steven put his college books down as he said, "I wish I could have kissed you out there on the street." Then he stood in front of Mark as his lover replied, "Well! Were not in the streets now, are we?" But Steven stopped him from taking him in his arms and quickly undid Mark's shirt instead, saying, "Wait! I've got a much better idea! Get all these clothes off and Ill show you!" Mark immediately stripped naked, then Steven lay him on the bed, having eagerly stripped himself as well.

Starting at Mark's forehead, Steven then kissed every inch of Mark's naked body, even his toes. Needless to say, this instantly developed into a full-blown sex session. Something that neither of them in any way objected to, naturally. Later that evening, once they had fully recovered from their love-making, they took a bath together, dressed in their best clothes, and went out to a restaurant for dinner, to celebrate Mark's good fortune. Though this did mean that Mark had to curb his lust in the mornings when he had to get to work, and it wasn't just Steven having to get to college. But neither of them minded that so much, it just meant that they were all the randier for each other when they got home.

In the evenings when Mark came home from work, they shared the chores of cooking, washing-up and keeping the room clean and tidy. That done, they then relaxed in front of the TV, or listened to music. Mark even helped Steven with his course-work for college. Then at bedtime, they either enjoyed a hot, rampant sex session, or just held each other tenderly before falling asleep, safe, and totally contented. To all outward appearances they were just two young men who shared a room together, and no-one gave them a second thought.

But, once they were alone in their little love-nest, the masks they wore outside came off, and they were free to express their love for each other in any way they wanted. Their sex was certainly never conventional either, and could happen at any time, whenever one of them was feeling horny. Something that they both really liked. But after they had lived together for some months, Steven came home from visiting his mother one Saturday evening. No sooner had he walked in the door, than Mark pounced on him, toppling him onto the bed and pinning him down as he kissed him passionately.

Steven really loved it when Mark handled him roughly, and he got turned-on instantly. Laying prone on the bed, Steven was perfectly happy to let his lover roughly strip him out of his clothes, his cock already rigid and slapping madly against his gently rising and falling stomach. But suddenly Mark took Steven's sweaty T-shirt, quickly rolled it up lengthways, and used it to blindfold him with, tieing it tightly at the back of his head so that he could then see absolutely nothing. Steven gasped, "Mark, you kinky fucker what are you up to!" But Mark didn't answer. Instead he took this opportunity to really torment Steven by getting off the bed, then suddenly, and without any warning, licking or caressing a different part of his horny body each time he touched him. Mark kept up this torment until Steven was gasping and moaning with desire, not knowing where Mark would strike next. It was then that he sprung his main surprise on his lover.

Laying there, his arms and legs spread wide in absolute surrender, his cock raging in its hardness, Steven then heard what sounded like Mark getting something out from under the bed. Then a few seconds later, Mark got on the bed and straddled his horny body as he kissed him passionately. When their lips parted, Mark said sexily, "No Steven! *You're* the kinky fucker." And before Steven could answer, Mark grabbed him roughly and dragged him off the bed onto the floor. Forcing Steven up onto his knees he then untied the blindfold to whip it off his head.

Steven's eyes shot open wide and his mouth dropped as he saw what stood on the carpet before him. Gazing up at Mark in disbelief, he pointed to the folded sheet of heavy-duty black plastic, and a can of motor-oil gasping, "You mean you're willing to do this? Just for me?" Nodding Mark replied, "Yes! Why not? But I'm sorry it could only be new motor-oil. Only I don't know any garage mechanics!" Scrambling to his feet Steven wrapped his arms around him and kissed him lovingly, as he kept repeating, "Thank you! Thank you," All the time, hardly able to believe this sign of Mark's love for him. Hurriedly they both pushed the chairs back against the wall and spread the plastic sheeting across the carpet.

Mark had also bought a plastic funnel, and had washed out an empty washing-up liquid bottle. Taking the cap off the bottle and putting the funnel into it, Mark then opened the can of oil and carefully filled the bottle with the clear light-brown liquid, whose smell was already affecting Steven remarkably. This done, Mark placed the bottle in the centre of the sheet. Then, with the can safely put to one side, Steven suggested that they both kneel at opposite sides of the sheet facing each other, with the bottle between them. Both their cocks were already hard, and Steven looked at Mark in lust-filled admiration as he said, "On a count of three, we both make a dive for the bottle! Whoever gets hold of it first, then has to try and spray the other with oil! But say I get the bottle first, while I'm trying to spray you with it, you have to try and turn the bottle around and spray me – OK!"

Naturally, this was a cause for much laughter as they both play-wrestled on the sheet of plastic, each determined to cover the other with oil first. Mark also found to his great surprise, that this kinky sex really turned him on, a lot more than he had at first thought it would. No sooner was the bottle empty, and their sexy young bodies were both covered in oil, than they eagerly set about smearing the slippery liquid all over each other, as their noses filled with the heady aroma given off by their sweating bodies. Then they slithered around in each others arms kissing and fondling each other, until Steven gasped, "Fuck me, you sexy bastard! Fuck me hard! Ram that fucking big cock up me!" Mark did just that, being much rougher in his handling of Steven than during their usual love-making.

They were both filled with a burning lust, but this turn-on was much heavier and very different for Mark as he experienced passions that were very new indeed, as he pulled and twisted Steven around into many different positions and fucked him hard, almost violently, both of them shooting their loads three or four times before they finally collapsed in heavenly bliss and complete exhaustion; their lust fully spent, their desire satiated.

From then on, this kinky sex was quite often repeated, and each time they enjoyed themselves to the full. Slithering around on the sheet, both of them gasping and moaning in their lust. Mark filling Steven's hungry arse with his hot sperm, while Steven shot his own repeatedly over both of their oil-slicked and sweating bodies. Then as they lay in each others arms, their heaving young bodies covered in oil, sweat and spunk, it was not uncommon for them both to just fall asleep where they lay. Once or twice when this happened, neither of them woke until early in the morning.

In a daze they then slithered around trying to get into the bathroom to wash themselves clean. Then they knocked into each other in their haste to get the sheet cleaned and put away under the bed with the oil, get their clothes on, gulp down some coffee, and run out of the door. Marks acceptance, and as it seemed, his full enjoyment of Steven's kink bringing them both even closer together, if indeed that were possible: they were so completely in love already.

Once they had been living together for six months, and fully established in their relationship, they decided that it was time for them to go out and start mixing with other gays, perhaps make new friends, who would accept them as a couple, and with whom they could enjoy socialising. During the time they had been apart, and once Mark had come to terms with his sexuality, he had become a regular visitor to the gay pubs and clubs in their hometown. Therefore, he knew only too well the ones to avoid. As he explained to Steven, quite often the people who went to some of these places, would take any opportunity they could find to try and split up a couple. And just because they had no stable relationship of their own.

At first Steven was really shocked to learn this, but he readily agreed with Mark that there was no way he wanted to meet those sort of people. Mark then told him of a nice, friendly club that he knew, where the members were mainly couples. But where even the majority of single men who went there, had a healthy respect for relationships, and wouldn't try their luck just because they might fancy one of the partners. This was called The

22 Club. It was jointly owned and run by Ron and Tony, who had been together for about fifteen years. And Mark told Steven that while Ron and Tony aimed to always create a warm and friendly atmosphere, they certainly wouldn't stand for anyone, regular or visitor, trying to cause any problems between a couple. And if necessary they would even throw them out if they had to.

They decided to visit the club on Saturday night, but Steven said, "The problem is, I've never been to these places before, and I suppose the other men will all be dressed up. I don't want to look plain when you'll probably be dressed up as well, because I wouldn't want you to be ashamed of me." Mark said simply, "I could never be ashamed of you Steven! But if you like, we can go shopping on Saturday afternoon, and find you something nice to wear. How does that sound?" Steven agreed that was a good idea, and so on Saturday afternoon he and Mark went shopping. They had a lot of fun doing this; Mark was acting the fool and making Steven laugh all the time. But he also kept a careful eye on the things that Steven looked at, noticing in one shop in particular, that his eyes lit up when he saw a blue silk shirt that Mark instantly thought would make him look really sexy. But immediately Steven looked away and started going through much cheaper shirts, which Mark knew was perfectly natural seeing that his lover only had his meagre college grant to live on.

Mark on the other hand had his inheritance and a good wage, and besides, he wanted Steven to look really sexy when they went to the club, so while Steven was busy looking for something cheaper, Mark quickly picked up one of the silk shirts, checked that it was the right size, and slipped quietly up to the cash-desk and paid for it. This done, he rejoined Steven who was having a hard time finding anything that he really liked.

Not wanting Steven to then spend money on another shirt, Mark said quietly in his ear, "Look, if you can't find anything you like, lets go home, and Ill find you something of mine to wear, OK? As far as I'm concerned I don't care what you wear! You always look sexy and good enough to eat, to me! And that's all I care about!" Reluctantly Steven agreed, though he really had wanted to look especially nice for Mark, when they went out to the club. On the way out of the shop he noticed the bag Mark was carrying, saying, "Have you bought something for yourself?" Keeping the bag away from him, Mark answered, "Yes, but it's only a white shirt for work. I needed a new one anyway." And no more was said about it.

That evening after dinner, they stripped and went into the bathroom to wash and get themselves ready. As they came back into their room to get dressed, Steven already excited about going out for the evening with Mark. He didn't notice that Mark went to the wardrobe and got out his best jeans for him, handing them to him and saying, "Here, sexy! Wear these tonight! And don't bother with any briefs!" Steven stared at him wide-eyed as he replied, "But Mark, you know these jeans fit so perfectly they show everything!" Mark just leered at him as he answered, "Yes! I know! That way there'll be less for me to strip off you when we get home, you sexy little beast!" And he took Steven in his arms and pretended to start eating his neck. Steven laughed and broke away. Then as he slid his jeans on, Mark quickly got into his own, also without any briefs.

Looking sexy enough already, Mark told Steven to lay down across the bed. More than happy to have another trick played on him, Steven did as he was told, and lay down with his arms spread wide. Mark then made a show of bringing out his own fashionable shirts that he always wore when going clubbing. First he brought out one and walking over to the bed, laid it across Steven's body and stood back. Then he pulled a face saying, "No! That's not really you Steven!" Before he brought out another and another, some of them being shirts that Steven really liked! But he lay there patiently, wanting Mark to decide exactly what he would wear that evening, and when Mark had laid eight different shirts, some of them very expensive shirts, over his prone body, then stood back again and pulled the same face, saying, "No, sorry Steven! Not one of those looks really right on you!" Steven was starting to get worried that he'd end up going to the club wearing nothing more exciting than a normal white T-shirt!

Gauging his moment perfectly, Mark shrugged his shoulders and said, "Look Steven. I've got an ordinary blue shirt left in the wardrobe. Wear that. It'll still look sexy on you. Anything does – even motor-oil!" Steven laughed, though inside he was really feeling disappointed that Mark didn't think any of those other beautiful shirts would look right on him. But Mark had always been right in everything else that he'd said so far, so Steven lay where he was, while Mark picked up the shirts, still on their hangers, and carried them back to the wardrobe. Then before he turned around he said, "Roll onto your belly, I want to try this against your shoulders to make sure it isn't too big for you!"

Steven immediately turned over and lay with his head buried in the pillows which was just perfect for what Mark wanted. Slipping the silk shirt off its hanger, he came back over to the bed and carefully let the shirt float down onto Steven's warm back. The feel of the silk on his skin was electric. Steven gasped, "Oh Mark! That feels so beautiful! Please let me try it on! Please! It feels so sexy!" Mark giggled, saying "Not half as sexy as you'll look in it tonight, you horny animal! Get up and Ill put it on for you!" Getting off the bed Steven turned around. His eyes nearly popped out of his head, when he saw Mark holding open the very shirt he had drooled over so badly in the shop. "B-but Mark! How?" He exclaimed, stumbling over his tongue in his excitement.

Mark silenced him, saying, "Shut up and slide your arms into it! When I saw the way you looked at it in the shop, I knew then just how sexy you'd look in it! So while you were looking at the cheaper shirts, I slipped this one up to the cash-desk and bought it for you!" Steven blinked, his mouth open wide, "For me! You mean you actually bought this for me!" And he threw his arms around Mark and hugged him really tight saying, "Oh Mark! Thank you! Thank you! I think it's really wonderful!"

When Mark finally got him to stand still so that he could fasten up the buttons, he then opened the front of Steven's jeans and tucked the shirt inside, making sure to flounce it out over the waistband, making Steven look really stunning. Steven whispered, "I love you Mark! And I'm going to feel really proud to be out with you tonight, wearing this beautiful shirt! When we come home, I hope that you'll fuck my arse all night long, 'till both of us flake out. It's the only way I can ever think of saying thank you for buying me something as beautiful, and expensive as this!" Taking him in his arms Mark kissed him tenderly, feeling the full force of his love for Steven surging up inside him.

Staring deeply into Steven's eyes he replied, "Having your love means more to me than fucking your arse Steven! I was a stupid arse-hole to run out on you in the first place! And to have a second chance with you – with someone so beautiful and sexy, so loving and genuine, means more to me than all the world! And while you're still at college, you mustn't ever feel ashamed that I have more money than you do, just because I'm working. So I decided today, on the way home, that from now on, we'll put our money together, every last penny! Your grant and my wages! And when either of us wants something, we can have it!" He kissed him again, then added, "Now stand back and let me really look at you! But I warn you – if you look too drop-dead-gorgeous, we might not even get out of the door tonight! Okay!" Steven groaned at the thought, but as Mark stood back and gazed at him lovingly, he said softly, "You know I always want to be naked and horny for you Mark! But it does seem a shame not to show this beautiful shirt off, now that you've bought it for me!" Laughing together, Mark groped the nice bulge Steven's cock was making down the left leg of his jeans. Then they quickly finished getting dressed and left for the club, both of them feeling happy and proud as they walked down the road together.

Reaching the club and stepping inside, Steven was immediately struck by the warm and friendly atmosphere. They were both warmly welcomed by Ron and Tony, who naturally remembered Mark. In fact, on being introduced to Steven, they both commented that he looked really stunning in his beautiful silk shirt. The moment Mark told them that they had been lovers for the last six months, Ron insisted that their first drinks were on the house, as he congratulated them both on their relationship. Many of the regulars also remembered Mark, and greeted him with warmth and sincerity, some even saying how they had missed seeing him for so long and asking where he had been hiding. But as soon as he introduced Steven as his boyfriend, they quickly understood his long absence.

As for Steven, he was quite amazed at how people just accepted him as Marks lover. So he was immediately able to feel truly relaxed and at ease. Over the last six months, while Mark had continued to point out to Steven that he certainly didn't profess to be an expert on gay sexuality, he had opened his eyes a lot to the varying types of gay men there were. But this was really Steven's first experience of mixing with other gay men. His first chance to really see for himself that they really weren't any different to him.

Feeling comfortable in the friendly surroundings of the club, Steven thoroughly enjoyed his evening. He danced with Mark several times, and even once or twice with a couple of other young men. And by the time they left the club, they had been given no less than six invitations, one each for Sunday lunch the next day and the following Sunday, and the rest for supper on various evenings over the next two weeks.

As they walked home together, Steven thought over what he had learned in the club. He was certainly even more comfortable now with the fact that it was normal for him to love Mark, live with him, and enjoy all the sex they shared. But it was still very strange to him, to actually be somewhere and see other men with their boyfriends. All of them perfectly happy and relaxed together.

At long last he began to feel that he really belonged somewhere, that amongst the people he'd met in the club at least, he was accepted completely as one of them. And he knew then, that they too all had exactly the same feelings and emotions as himself.

From the time when he and Mark had first started playing around together, even moreso once he met and fell in love with Paul, he had been very aware that the things he both enjoyed and which truly excited him, others thought of as filthy and disgusting! Even unnatural and perverted! And Paul had gone to a lot of trouble to make him understand that others would think these things about him, if they were ever to find out what they did together. Therefore, there had never been anyone before, that he could talk to about his feelings and desires, and so he had always felt very alone and isolated. Only on his regular visits to the garage had he been able to come alive and really be himself. But now he had Mark, and he knew that they were both secure and comfortable in their love for each other.

They had discovered that they both shared the same kink and often talked openly and without any shame, about possible ways of developing it. Discussing how to make their sex-lives even more enjoyable for both of them. They even discussed the possibility of sharing their sex with someone else. And how they would both feel about it. If they met the right person that was! And having been to the club and seen other couples just like him and Mark, he was beginning to realise that it really doesn't matter what others said or thought about him in their ignorance! All that truly mattered is that he was always true to Mark and to himself.

Five

On a Saturday evening some two months after Steven's first visit to the gay club, he had been round to visit his mother. He returned home just after eight o'clock, and had been surprised when he glanced up from the street to see that there were no lights on in their room. Wondering where Mark could have gone, he had just opened the door to their room and was about to reach for the light-switch, when the lights came on, and there was a rousing chorus of HAPPY BIRTHDAY TO YOU .... filling the room. He stood there in absolute shock and amazement, as he saw all their new friends, with Mark standing right there in front of them, all of them in party mood.

It was his twentieth birthday and although he had hoped that Mark would buy him something, he had no idea that anything like this was being planned! Mark, with a broad grin on his face, came forward, wrapped his arms around him and gave him a big birthday kiss, much to the delight and approval of all the other guests. Each of them congratulated him in turn and kissed him. He was overwhelmed by the love and warmth that filled him, and he had to fight very hard to hold back the tears of pure joy that quickly welled up in his eyes.

Mark then led him over to a table, as the guests all parted to let them through. Once there, Steven's eyes nearly popped out of his head, when he saw a small mountain of presents, all for him! Whispering in his ear, Mark asked him to open Ron and Tony's present first, explaining that they would have to leave early to open the club, but that neither of them wanted to miss his party. It was a big package, and once Steven tore open the wrapping-paper, he was totally speechless! There, on the table, was the very latest mini-hi-fi, and with it, five of his favourite CDs. Steven just couldn't believe his eyes! He'd had no idea that they thought so much about him! Immediately he hugged and kissed them both in turn. Stumbling over his words in his haste to thank them sincerely. But the look of pure joy in his eyes was for them, thanks enough.

Next he opened David and Richard's present and found again to his delight, that it contained three more CD's, and a video that he had wanted for ages. They were a really nice couple, and had been together for the last three years. The four of them often went out for a meal or to the cinema together. After hugging, kissing and thanking them both, he then opened Stuarts present, which was a new shirt. It was pale green, his favourite colour. Stuart was one of their few single friends, but they knew that he cared about them both, and their happiness. So to them, he was just as special as the others.

He opened Paul's present next. Paul was another single young man who was just eighteen. He was a very lonely person, who found it hard to be gay because of his homophobic parents. So he often liked to come around and talk with them, knowing that he could relax and be himself. His present was a small bottle of rather expensive aftershave and, when Steven hugged and kissed him, he whispered in his ear, "Thanks a lot Paul, but you shouldn't have spent so much money!" He play-punched Paul in the stomach, and they both laughed. The rest of his presents included, more toiletries, socks, and another shirt, but he noticed with a slight tinge of disappointment, that there was no present from Mark. But he quickly dismissed this from his mind, thinking that after all, Mark had organised this wonderful party for him, which must have taken a lot of work. Besides, what did he need presents from his boyfriend for, when he had all of his love.

Soon the party was in full swing, and Steven noticed that there was plenty of lovely things to eat and drink. But one of the many things he had already learned about gays, was that they certainly knew how to throw a party! He and Mark having been invited to many over the last two months. Everyone thoroughly enjoyed themselves, and Steven had a wonderful time and was very grateful to Mark for having arranged it all for him. He even got a little drunk, which was very unusual for him. But then so did everyone else, so no-one noticed.

It was four o'clock on Sunday morning when the party finally broke up and they were almost alone again. Paul was the last to leave, and being a little the worse for drink, was hugging, and kissing them both with a lot more passion than he normally did. He was tall and very slender and they both thought he was very sexy. They had seen him naked many times already, though they hadn't had sex with him. They had met him one night in the club,

taking to him at once and telling him that he could come and visit them whenever he wanted to.

When he had first started coming around, he had always asked at the
door, if it was all right to come in and stay with them for a while?' adding that
he didn't want to be in the way. But seeing his need to feel wanted, neither of
them minded having him around. And after his first few visits they were
pleased to see him begin to feel more and more relaxed and natural around
them, almost like a part of the family. He had told them openly that he'd had
very little sexual experience, so to help him gain confidence, they both decided that when either or both of them wanted to have a bath, they would just go
ahead and strip naked in front of him.

At first, Paul was embarrassed about this, but once he saw how natural
they were about being naked in front of him, one evening he just turned
around and asked, "I'm feeling really sweaty! Is it all right if I have a bath?",
to which they naturally agreed. So a little nervously he had stripped naked in
front of them. From then on it had become perfectly natural for at least one of
them to be naked at some time or other during his long visits.

Feeling Paul's hard cock sticking into him, Steven glanced at Mark ques-
tioningly. Mark just nodded and whispered in his ear, "Why not?" So Steven
started undoing the buttons of Paul's shirt, while Mark moved around behind
him, pressing his own hardening cock against Paul's firm round arse as he
slipped his hands around Paul's slender waist and started to undo his belt and
then the front of his jeans. Steven said softly, "Paul, it really was good of you
to buy me that great aftershave. But it really is too late for you to go home
now, and we both feel that there's another present under these clothes
somewhere, that you'd really like to give us? Don't you think we'd better get
you out of these clothes and make you feel better! How do you feel about that,
sexy?"

By then Steven had Paul's shirt open, off his shoulders, and was sliding
it down his arms, which hung limply at his sides. While Mark had Paul's jeans
and boxers down around his ankles, and was slipping his shoes off, to get his
jeans and boxers off over his feet. Paul's solid eight-inch cock was slapping
against his smooth stomach, the head already oozing pre-cum as he sighed
deeply, then said softly, "I've been wanting the two of you to do this to me for

ages! But I didn't have the nerve to ask you, with you two being boyfriends and everything! I thought if I did, you might not let me come around here any-more!"

He kissed Steven passionately, while letting them both strip him com-pletely. Then he turned around and kissed Mark, before looking from one to the other and smiling sheepishly, said, "I really love the feel of your hands on my body! You can both do anything you want to me! Now! And anytime I come around! I love you both! And having seen your sexy bodies naked loads of times, the thought of being able to actually have sex with you, and not lose your friendship, is just wicked! Fuck! This has got to be the best night of my entire life!" Mark locked the door, and they walked him over to the bed as they quickly shed their own clothes.

Once they were also naked, the three of them got onto the bed together. Immediately hands and mouths explored every piece of naked flesh they could find, all three of them driving each other wild with lust. And they were both very pleased to see that just like them, Paul gave full reign to his lust and passion too. So neither Steven or Mark felt in the least guilty in having sex with Paul, because to them, he really was like a part of the family. And they had made the decision together, so they knew it was what they both wanted.

After much kissing, caressing, cocksucking and ball and arse licking, the three of them ended up with Paul stretched out on his back, legs and arms spread wide in complete abandon. Steven straddled Paul's smooth slender body and rode up and down on his rigid cock. Mark fed his solid cock all the way down Paul's very cock-hungry throat and fucked his mouth at the same time. And from the moans and sighs that kept coming from him, they were in no doubt at all that he was loving it all just as much as they were.

Having filled Paul's mouth with hot sperm, while Steven milked his young balls of their full load, they then slid him around so that his head was hanging over the edge of the bed. Mark then got between Paul's legs, folding them right back against his still-heaving chest, and before he knew it, Mark had greased his still-rampant cock and slid it all the way up his arse, while Steven stood beside the bed and fed Paul his own engorged shaft, which Paul sucked and slurped on greedily. Paul was more than willing to surrender his horny young body to his two fantastic friends, and again he moaned and sighed deeply as they fucked his arse and mouth at the same time, holding themselves back all the time, to make sure he got the very best sex of his life. And when neither of them could hold back any longer, they filled him at both ends with even more delicious, creamy spunk, hearing him sighing deeply with contentment as he guzzled it down.

Exhausted, the three of them then got under the covers with Paul on his back in the middle, and cuddled up to each other. And as they all started to drift off to sleep, Paul was still mumbling his thanks for being allowed to stay with them, and have their wonderful hard cocks make him feel so wanted.

They both kissed him on the cheek at the same time, their hands running softly over his body as he lay between them. Sighing contentedly, Paul said, "You two have always really made me feel that it's all right to be gay! Not like my parents! Being here with you two, is the only place where I ever really feel wanted! As me I mean! And now, I hope there'll be lots more times when I come round, that you'll just strip me naked, and do all these wonderful things to me again! Not all the time! Only when you both want to, I mean! And I hope, that one day, I'll be lucky enough to meet a Steven or a Mark of my own, who'll make me feel this good!"

Squeezing him tight, Steven said softly, "We both love you Paul, and whenever you're feeling horny and frustrated, all you have to do is say the word, and we'll be happy to do this with you, anytime you want it!" Paul just exclaimed, "Wow! That's really neat! But I liked it just then, when you both got me and stripped me! Maybe I just like to be taken, I don't know! But that's the way I'd like you two to do it, when you want my dick or my arse! Is that okay?" Having the same idea, they both reached between his legs. Steven squeezed Paul's cock which was hard again, while Mark squeezed his balls. Paul gasped and thrust his hips forward off the bed as he moaned, "Hmmm! That feels nice! Do it a bit harder, please!"

Suddenly neither of them felt tired anymore; seeing a new side to Paul that they'd had no way of knowing existed before. Both squeezing even harder, Steven sucked hard on Paul's left nipple and Mark quickly did the same with the other. Gasping and panting, Paul thrust his young supple body up and down on the bed between them, showing them that they were affecting him in a completely new and different way. As they both saw how much he was turned-on by this heavy handling, it wasn't long before Steven and Mark had him up on his hands and knees. Mark sliding his solid cock in and out of Paul's arse once again, as he slapped Paul's firm round arse-cheeks hard with his hands.

Steven also fed his rigid cock in and out of Paul's slurping mouth, while he teased his firm proud nipples between his fingers. Paul was quickly spaced out by this treatment and moaned and sighed deeply as his young body was tormented mercilessly with the wonderful mixture of searing pain and unspeakable pleasure. And Paul slid his mouth off Steven's solid cock just for a second to gasp, "More! More! Do it harder!" Then he buried his mouth back on the cock that he loved so much. Steven and Mark both kept up their rough handling of Paul's willing and eager body, while they fucked him really hard at both ends. Letting him fully experience what may well be turning out to be the birth of his own kink. And by the time they both fired their hot sperm inside his trembling body, they knew that Paul would indeed be a regular and willing guest in their bed from then on.

Mark and Paul woke first. It was midday, and they silently crept out of bed and Mark got Paul to help him tidy up all the mess from the party. They both stayed naked and worked as silently as they could, leaving the Birthday Boy in Dreamland. Then after drinking some coffee and eating some of the left-over sandwiches, at Marks direction they both picked up their clothes and silently slipped out of the room and went into the bathroom. They bathed together, another new experience for Paul, and Mark treated him to a morning blow-job before they both got dressed and Paul went home, while Mark went out to do something himself.

It was two o'clock when Mark returned, to find Steven still sound asleep. Waking him gently with a kiss, he stroked his hair and said, "How do you feel, Birthday-Boy?" Steven looked into his lover's eyes and answered, "Wonderful! Just wonderful!" He stretched his lithe body in the bed, almost making Mark forget his purpose. Then he asked, "Has Paul gone home?" Mark smiled and nodded. Steven asked, "How was he this morning? Not feeling guilty I hope?" Mark kissed him again, then replied, "Paul was fine! Look – he even helped me tidy up the mess from the party when we got up this morning!"

Laying down beside Steven he kissed him again, then he went on, "After the work was done, we had some coffee and some of the left-over sandwiches. Then I took him into the bathroom and we had a bath together!" He laughed, then went on, "You should have seen the look of wonder on his face! I'll bet he's never had a bath with anyone else before! And to make sure there were no nagging doubts in his mind, I gave him a morning blow-job as well, before we both got dressed. Then he went off home looking as happy and relaxed as I've ever seen him!" Slipping his left hand under the covers, Mark soon found Steven's hard cock and wrapped his fingers around it as he sighed, saying, "You are so beautiful, all I really want to do right now is get these clothes off, get back into bed with you, and eat you alive!" Steven smiled at him.

But Mark pulled his hand from under the covers as in a much sharper tone he snapped, "But that will have to wait! Get up and get dressed! I know you were disappointed last night, when you thought I hadn't bought you a present! Even though you did try hard not to show it! Come on, lazy-bones! Throw some clothes on and come with me!" And he stood up and half-dragged Steven out of bed, ignoring all his protestations and questions as to what on earth Mark was up to.

Stumbling into his jeans and new silk shirt, Steven just had time to slip on his trainers before Mark grabbed him by the hand and dragged him out of the door and down the stairs; Mark still ignoring Steven's questions and pleas as to be told what this was all about. Once outside the front door, Mark then led him straight down the side of the house, to the garage which was built towards the back of the building, just in front of the garden. But before he opened the doors he took from his pocket a large mustard bandana, and this he quickly rolled up and tied around Steven's head as a blindfold. Steven was already bursting with curiosity as to why Mark had led him out here of all places! What had happened? Surely if aliens had landed there the noise would have woken him up! But soon Marks strange behaviour was made clear to him, as Mark led him inside the garage, closed the doors behind them, and removed the blindfold.

Steven just stood there, glued to the spot in both shock and utter amazement. There, right before his eyes, stood a sparkling, brand new Honda 500 motorbike. His mouth fell open and his eyes nearly popped out of his head! He was completely lost for words! They had both recently learned to ride motorbikes. Their friend Alex had one, and he had taught them. Steven had even passed his test and had his full license.

Since Alex had first offered to teach them, they had often talked about how good it would be to have a bike of their own. Then they could get out into the country at weekends or during the holidays. They had also both joked about what the feel of the throbbing machine between their legs would do to them. But Steven had never imagined in his wildest dreams that Mark would go and do something like this. Standing beside him, Mark slipped his arm around Steven's waist as he said quietly, "This is for you, with all my love".

Steven turned to him and immediately threw his arms around his neck and squeezed him tight as he gasped, "Oh Mark! Thank you! Thank you! Its the most wonderful surprise I've ever had!" He kissed him several times, then went on, "I love you! I love you more than anyone else in the whole wide world, and I always will!" Then their lips met again, and they kissed with a passion and urgency that carried the full force of their love behind it. Naturally their cocks automatically shot to full hardness between them. But before either of them got carried away, Mark broke the kiss saying wide-eyed, "And there's more!"

Steven stared at him in wonder, as he thought what else could Mark possibly have bought for him. And he was completely dumbfounded when Mark brought out from a hiding place, first a pair of tight, black leather trousers, followed by a black leather motorbike jacket, and a pair of proper leather motorbike boots.

Laying the leather trousers and jacket across the seat of the bike, he placed the boots beside it on the floor, then smiled at his lover as he said, "Come on Steven! Strip off and put these on. Then we can go out for a ride!" But the smile soon faded on Marks face when he saw the worried look on Steven's. "But Mark!" Steven exclaimed, "All this must have cost you a fortune! Where on earth did you get all this money from? Oh please! Don't think that I'm ungrateful! This is all so wonderful! But how could you possibly afford all this?"

The smile returned to Marks face again as he answered, "You silly sod!

For a second there, I thought that you didn't like my surprise! You know that you leave all the finances to me! Well! When I saw the look in your eyes every time you went out on Alex's bike, I decided that as your birthday was coming up, if I couldn't dip into my inheritance to buy something really special for the one person who means the whole world to me, then what was the point of me having the fucking money in the first place! As for the leather gear and the boots, when I told your mum what I was planning, she said that shed pay half towards them! That's why there was no present from her! I just told you that we had to call round and see her today to collect your present, to save spoiling the surprise! Now, worry-guts, will you strip, and let me see how good you look in leather?"

Feeling very ashamed and embarrassed that he hadn't trusted Mark totally, Steven quickly stripped naked, and Mark folded his clothes and put them into one of the bags from the leather shop. Then he said, "Those leather trousers should be skin-tight. Just wait till you feel them next to your bare skin!" And he gave an impish grin. Steven eagerly worked his body into them, finding that indeed they were very tight, and stiff too, with the leather being new. But he was also amazed at how sexy they felt around his arse and his crotch.

Next he slid his bare feet into the boots and Mark helped him fasten them up. Last of all he put on the leather jacket. This was quilted inside and at once made him feel warm and comfortable. Mark wolf-whistled in sheer admiration. Only then did Steven notice that Mark had also shed his clothes, and was quickly climbing into matching leathers, just like his! This made Steven's cock twitch inside his new leather trousers, and he returned the wolf-whistle, groping his crotch, to show his appreciation. When they were both fully dressed Mark brought out two matching white crash-helmets that were really shiny, and had tinted visors. Handing one to Steven, he slid his own over his head. Then they wheeled the bike out of the garage and Steven mounted it and started the engine. The feeling of the machine throbbing between his young thighs was electric! And as soon as Mark climbed on behind him, Steven opened the throttle and they sped down the drive, then they were off down the road, gliding smoothly through the light Sunday traffic, heading out of town for the open country.

The bike purred sweetly as they sped along the country roads. The constant throb of the engine between their legs having had its effect on cocks even before they cleared the town, so that they were both suffering raging hard-ons, and Steven's arse was twitching like anything. The country roads were deserted, so Mark reached around Steven's body and slid his right hand down between his outstretched legs, groping his aching cock through the tight leather and moulding it with his fingers. Then sliding his left hand up Steven's body, he pulled down the zip on Steven's jacket and slipped his hand inside, where he played with his nipples, which were already firm and erect. For both of them these new sensations were mind-blowing, and their lust for each other was soon becoming unbearable as the miles sped by. But they carried on riding for as long as they could, until Steven couldn't stand it any longer and slowed the bike down as they came to a small wood, and he turned off the road into it.

Carefully, they rode the bike deeper into the wood until they were sure they wouldn't be seen by any passing motorists. Then Steven turned off the engine and they both dismounted and pulled the bike up onto its stand and took off their helmets. These they lay carefully on the ground, and the next second, they were locked in a passionate embrace. Their tongues darting in and out of each others mouths, their hands roaming everywhere.

They were both amazed at just how desperate they were for each other. Almost as if they had never had sex together before. Their cocks were raging in their hardness, and completely disregarding their surroundings, they both worked feverishly to get each other naked, their throbbing cocks bouncing around in the air, slapping against their heaving stomachs, as a desperate ache filled them both, and they yearned to possess each other completely.

Mark told Steven to mount the bike facing backwards, so that he could then lay back with his neck against the handlebars and his legs spread wide. Steven did this at once. Then Mark straddled the bike facing him, and at once he bent forward, devouring Steven's cock in one deep thrust, sliding it all the way down his hungry throat until Steven's balls rested against his chin. Then he started a magical blow-job that was so powerful that it had Steven writhing about, gasping and moaning as he flailed his arms and legs helplessly in the air, almost threatening to dislodge it from its stand.

He sucked and massaged Steven's cock with his hot mouth and tongue so expertly that every stroke was driving him wild, and he kept this up until he felt Steven's balls begin to tighten in their sack. Only then did he ease off to stop Steven from tipping over the edge and delivering his load.

Many times Mark repeated this manoeuvre, his every action calculated to drive Steven insane with lust. Finally Steven was begging and pleading with him to stop and fuck the hell out of him, panting desperately, "Oh Mark! I can't stand it any more! Fold my legs back and fuck the arse off me! Please! I haven't felt this fucking horny since I used to see Paul the mechanic! Oh please ram your cock up me! Please! I'm really desperate for it! Or turn me over so my arse is up in the air and really shaft me till I drop! Please! I'm begging you!"

Of course this was exactly what Mark had been aiming for. At once he got off the bike and told Steven to turn over, and put both of his arms on the handlebars so he could rest his head on them. Then he got him to lift his sweet young arse high in the air, his legs spread wide on either side of the bike. Mark then got back on the bike, reaching down to open a small compartment just above the rear wheel. From this he produced a small can of axle-grease, which he smeared on his cock before working some into Steven's desperate fuck-hole. Then just as he started to slide his cock all the way up his lovers hungry arse, he held the can under Steven's nose. Steven went wild.

As Mark fucked him, so Steven lifted his arse, pushing backwards to meet every thrust and drive his lovers cock even deeper into him. All the time Steven was moaning and gasping for air, completely lost in the ecstasy of sensations that flooded the whole of his horny and sweating young body. Not only was he out of his mind with lust over having Marks rigid cock thrusting forcefully in and out of his hungry arse, but there was the rush he was getting from the smell of the axle-grease, and something completely new! Then he realised what it was. They had put their new leathers across the bike and he was lying on them. Suddenly the smell and feel of the leather against his naked skin added to all the rest, was sending him into an delirium of absolute bliss.

Mark was also feeling the same heightening in his lust, as the feel and smell of the leather worked on his body too, and he drove his rigid cock in and out of Steven's arse with a force and urgency that he had never known before. Totally lost in their fucking, neither of them said anything about this, yet somehow they both seemed only too aware that they now had a new avenue to explore in their already fantastic sex-life. Stepping up his fucking pace as never before, Mark was sliding his whole shaft right out of Steven's gaping hole, then thrusting it back inside him again, almost sending Steven flying over the handlebars, so great was the energy he put into every thrust.

Steven responded to this much rougher treatment in a way that surprised even him. Suddenly he heard his own voice, but seeming as if it came from a long way off, shouting, "Yes! Yes! Fuck me harder! Really plough my fucking hole! Slap my arse too, as hard as you like! Oh fuck! I love it! I love it! Give it to me! Really fuck my brains out!" This resounded in Marks brain, urging him to hammer his painfully hard cock into Steven with all his strength. And without even thinking about it, he brought his right hand crashing down on Steven's right arse-cheek. Whack! Then again. Crack! Crack! At first Steven gasped as the intense pain penetrated his brain. But as Mark continued to rain down blow after blow, all the time keeping up his now almost vicious fucking, the delicious pain in his arse served only to increase his lust. In seconds he was shouting, "Yes! Oh Yes! Beat my tight arse! Harder! Harder! Beat it till its raw! Fuck me senseless! Hmmm! Oh yes! I really love it!"

They kept up this demented feverpitch for nearly an hour. Each feeding off the others new-found lust. Mark continued to rain down blows on Steven's already burning arse-cheeks, while all the time pounding his throbbing cock in and out of Steven's loosened arse, with more force than he had ever done before.

As for Steven, he continued to beg, plead and urge Mark to really hurt him, telling him how much he needed it. At the same time, he reached down and grabbed hold of his aching and long-ignored cock, fisting it with such force and intensity that it soon became sore. But this new pain only drove him on even more, and he stopped only momentarily to prevent himself from shooting his load, then started fisting it viciously all over again.

But finally, when neither of them could hold back any longer, Marks cock fired his pent-up load deep inside Steven's blazing and swollen arse. And Steven sent the biggest load of his life splattering across his sweat-drenched chest and stomach. Both totally exhausted and gasping for air, Steven collapsed forward, laying his head on his left arm while he massaged his sperm all over his body with his right hand and moaned deliriously. Mark just collapsed onto his back, and there they remained, neither of them able to move a muscle, as they both closed their eyes and drifted off to sleep. It had been perhaps the most powerful experience they had shared together. And one which they both knew they would come to develop, and enjoy all the more as time went by.

Six

Steven was the first to wake, and felt the heavy weight of Marks sleeping body pressing on his back. By then it must have been quite late, because all around them was dark and there was moonlight filtering through the trees, making everything appear slightly eerie. Semi-dazed, Steven lay still while trying to get his eyes accustomed to the darkness. Suddenly he shot fully awake, as he realised that one of the dark shapes near the bike was moving. His mind flashed back to that other wood, where the unknown man had fucked him in the mud. How the second man had crept up on him in the darkness and fucked him as well. And how he had finally seen yet another figure in the darkness, which had turned out to be Mark.

Just as he had on that other occasion, his eyes made out that the mystery figure had the front of his trousers open wide, and that he was stroking his solid engorged cock, right there in front of him. It was then that Steven remembered that he and Mark were both naked. But before Steven could do anything to rouse Mark, in a soft voice the stranger said, "Don't get worried! I don't mean no harm! I watched the two of you earlier, when you were having sex. WOW! Were you ever going at it! I shot two loads just watching you from behind one of the trees."

He came closer to the bike, still stroking his rigid erection. Steven turned on the bike's dipped headlights, and instantly he gasped and felt himself go cold all over. He stared at the stranger in total amazement. Not at the size of his cock, but because he was wearing a police uniform. Fully realising his and Marks nakedness, Steven was wondering what he could possibly do to explain their present state, when again it registered in his brain that the stranger was holding his rigid cock in his right hand.

Trying to hide the panic in his voice Steven said, "Are you a gay policeman?" The stranger laughed. Then he replied, "Oh! Sorry! I didn't mean to scare you! No. I'm not. I just like wearing this uniform! It really turns me on! I often bring it with me from the village and change into it when I get into the woods. Then I just walk around in it, until I feel really horny! Then I pull my dick out and fist it like fuck till I shoot my load! A couple of times I've caught other young men naked, here in the woods, having sex together. Then I pretended that I was a real copper! And all the time I was looking at their smooth, naked young bodies, and their really hard dicks, my own cock was aching like fuck inside my uniform trousers."

He laughed again, as he reached out and ran his free hand down over Marks bare back, right to his arse. Then he went on, "Its really amazing what young blokes will do in that situation, especially if they think by doing it, he's going to let them go!"

Having realised that he and Mark were safe, Steven began to feel his own cock stirring into life beneath him as he gazed down at the strangers hard seven-inch dick. He had never thought that he or Mark would want to have sex with anyone else, except perhaps with Paul that was. But already this had been a day of new experiences, and he could feel his mouth begin to water, as he looked at that delicious throbbing pole in the strangers hand.

Reaching out, the stranger took his own hand away and Steven folded his hand around the solid shaft. The stranger gasped at the contact and closed his eyes. Steven worked his hand up and down the pulsating shaft, as with his other hand he nudged Mark awake, saying, "Hey Mark! Wake up! We have a visitor – he needs attention!" Mark stirred. Then as the words slowly penetrated his brain, he sat up on the seat. Seeing the police uniform brought him fully awake, but Steven quickly reassured him saying, "Don't worry about the uniform! He's not a real copper! He says that he just likes wearing it. That it's a real turn-on for him. Apparently he was watching us from behind a tree when we were having sex, and he really got off on it." Seeing the strangers solid cock, with Steven's hand wrapped around the shaft, Marks own cock began to stiffen instantly.

Leaning forward, Mark whispered in Steven's ear, "Are you thinking what I'm thinking?", as he slowly massaged Steven's cock with his hand. Steven moaned as he said, "Well! I was thinking that this has been a day for new experiences! But only if we both want it!" Without another word, they both got off the bike. Standing in front of the stranger, with their hard cocks throbbing madly, Mark asked, "What's your name?" The stranger replied, "My names

Vince, short for Vincent!" Steven asked, "And how old are you Vince?"

Vince moaned as Steven pumped his aching cock with his hand. Then he answered, "I'm nineteen. But I live alone in a farm cottage about three miles from here!" He didn't say anything else, he just stood there as Steven and Mark slowly stripped him completely naked. Running their soft hands all over his smooth naked body, Vince whimpered as his body trembled under their touch. And when his head was spinning with lust he gasped, "Oh this is like a dream come true for me! And you two blokes are so fucking sexy! You can both do anything you want to me. Honest! Hmmm! Oh shit! Your hands running all over me like this, are making me as horny as fuck! Oooo yeah! Please don't stop till you've fucked me rotten! Please!" Silently Steven fell to his knees on the ground and sucked Vince's throbbing cock deep into his throat. Vince gasped and his entire body trembled even more.

While this was going on, Mark slipped behind Vince, running his hands all over his back until he was caressing his firm young arse-cheeks. Vince was moaning even louder by then, but when Mark slid down, parted his arse-cheeks, and began licking up and down his crack with his hot tongue, Vince gasped and wriggled his arse about in Marks face as he yelled, "Oh fuck! This is too much! Oh please shove your fucking hard dick up me! Please! Oh I've never felt anything this fantastic before!" But Steven and Mark were in no mood to hurry their enjoyment of Vince's hot and sexy young body. So they ignored his pleading, while Steven kept switching his attention between Vince's deliciously rigid and painfully hard cock, and his quite large balls, which he found he could only take into his warm wet mouth one at a time.

Nevertheless, he treated them both to a good hot suck, as he slavered all over them with his already expert tongue. But only a few more seconds of this proved to be too much for the country boy. His mouth open wide, head thrown right back, he let out a long, loud gasp, as his whole body shook under the violent sensations shooting through him while he emptied his full load deep into Steven's hungry throat. Though little did he know that was not to be the end of it!

By then, Mark had his hot tongue buried deep in Vince's fuck-hole, and was licking him out ferociously. In fact Vince's hole was then nicely open, and Marks own raging hard-on knew exactly where it was going. Getting to his feet, Mark signalled to Steven, and before Vince knew what was happening, they quickly laid him across the bike on his belly. Steven then grabbed the tin of axle-grease from the ground, handing this to Mark who dipped his fingers in it and got them nicely coated with the gooey stuff. Then he plastered his swollen cock with grease and at once presented the head to Vince's puckered and hungry fuck-hole.

Giving him no time to object, Mark pushed forward, and soon Marks solid shaft was buried to his balls in the warm tight arse of the beautiful farm-boy. At the same time, Steven went around to the other side of the bike, where he pressed his own aching hard cock against Vince's lips. Vince opened his mouth instantly and sucked Steven's cock inside, moaning with delight. With Marks cock buried all the way up his arse, and already starting to fuck him, and Steven's cock sliding smoothly in and out of his mouth, Vince's lust was in full control, and he relaxed his body completely and willingly let the pair of them fuck the hell out of him.

Pounding their rampant cocks in and out of Vince's mouth and arse, Steven and Mark leaned across his prone body and kissed, as their own lust soared heavenward. The fantastic fuck-session with Paul the night before, the smell and feel of their new leathers against their naked flesh, the constant throb of the bike between their legs, the smell of the axle-grease, and then meeting Vince like that, all combined to work on their senses, releasing inside them an almost animal passion, that their own kinks had so-far only shown them the merest glimpse of.

Again Steven picked up the tin of grease, which he first held under his nose while he breathed in deeply. All his senses went wild! Then he held the can under Marks nose as he fucked. The result was that they both started to fuck in and out Vince's helpless body like pneumatic rams, with almost no regard for the human being that was prone between them and completely at their mercy. While doing this, Steven dipped his fingers into the grease and smeared it all over his own body. Then he smeared some all over Mark, and all over Vince's back. Breathing in yet more of the warm scent from the grease coming off their hot and sweating young bodies, Mark began slapping Vince's arse quite hard, all the time keeping up the ferocity of his fucking, while Steven grabbed a handful of Vince's hair and used this as a handle to ram his face deeper and harder onto his aching cock.

Powerless though he was, at no time during their savage use of him did Vince make the slightest attempt to stop them. Mark was the first to reach his climax, and gasped and yelled as he lunged into Vince's arse with such force that it nearly knocked the bike off its stand. Trembling all over, he gasped and panted as he emptied his hot thick load of sperm deep inside Vince's raw and well-fucked arse. This in turn pushed Steven over the top, and he too buried his cock deep down Vince's throat and held his face hard against his crotch, while he pumped wad after hot wad of sticky, creamy spunk deep into Vince's heaving stomach. And being totally out of control, due to the vicious way that he had been used, Vince continued to slurp and suck on Steven's cock, until every last droplet of spunk was drained from Steven's balls, as he gasped and panted around the cock in his mouth and fired off his own second load all over the shiny new bike seat and his stomach. Only then did he let Steven's shrinking rod slip from his mouth.

Immediately Mark pulled Vince roughly upright, his own cock still hard and buried deep inside him. Grabbing Vince roughly at the back of his head, he pushed his face down onto the seat and shouted. "You filthy animal! This is a brand new bike! Lick all that spunk up, fuck-boy! Or I'll fuck you so hard, you'll never sit down again!" The fierceness and anger in Marks voice even made Steven jump. Vince reacted immediately, and lapped at the seat with his tongue. But to help him in this, Steven took hold of a clump of Vince's hair again, and wiped his face backwards and forwards through the sperm as Vince was trying to lick it up, so that his face soon became covered in it too! And he kept that up until every trace of sperm was gone.

Mark also punished Vince by repeatedly slapping his already sore arse-cheeks really hard, to show him that he must never do that again. And only when Steven released Vince's hair did Mark finally slide his solid cock out of him. Coming around to join them, Steven collapsed on the ground with the other two and they all rested after their heavy session. After some time, Vince was the first to speak. As he gazed from one to the other in what could only have been deep admiration he said, "F-U-C-K! Was that ever heavy! I've sucked loads of stiff horny cocks! But I've never had anything like that happen to me before!" He chuckled to himself, then added softly, "Well! Only in my wildest fantasies, maybe! Tonight, you two have just made a dream come true for me. I really hope that we can stay friends, and see a lot more of each other. Shit! That was fucking brilliant!"

Once rested, they all started to feel the chill of the night air on their naked bodies, so Vince asked, "Hey! Why don't we all get dressed, and then the two of you can come back to my place and we can have some hot coffee and talk for a while? Get to know each other proper like!" This seemed like a good idea, so all three of them got up and started putting on their clothes. Or at least Steven and Mark did. Vince told them to wait there for him, and he walked off naked through the woods, saying as he went that he had to get his clothes from their hiding place. He returned a few minutes later, dressed in a T-shirt and jeans. Then, after folding up the police uniform, put it into a bag he had with him, and the three of them left the wood together, all three lending a hand to push the bike.

As they walked together, Vince explained that the cottage where he lived was some distance away from the main farmhouse, so it was completely private. He also explained that he had come to work on the farm a year ago, after being thrown out by his parents when they found out that he was gay. The cottage was very small, but they both noticed at once that everything was kept neat and tidy. There were two bedrooms; with a bathroom that had been built out of the largest one, which was on the left, at the top of the stairs.

The stairs themselves were steep and narrow; they effectively cut the cottage into two halves. Standing inside the front door, to the left of the stairs was a sitting room, and to the right the kitchen. As he showed them around, Vince explained that the farmer and his wife had been very good to him, once they saw what a good and willing worker he was. And they had made sure that the cottage had everything in it that he needed. And had told him that he could live his own life as he wanted to. Steven and Mark were quite impressed.

While they were all upstairs, standing in the spare bedroom, which was sparsely furnished with an old single bedstead, with an even older feather mattress, and a heavy wooden wardrobe, Vince suggested that they should strip naked, and wash off the grease, sperm and sweat that they were all covered in. Quickly they all stripped, and went into the small bathroom together to have a refreshing wash. But while it was perfectly natural that their cocks all automatically stood to attention as they washed and handled each others bodies, none of them were in the mood to start a new session at that moment. Instead they just horsed around, laughing and joking with each other, until they were all clean and dried-off. Then when they came out of the bathroom, they just left their clothes on the bed and went downstairs naked.

Working together, they made coffee and sandwiches in the kitchen, and then took these into the sitting room where they all laid on the carpet in front of the fire while they relaxed and enjoyed their supper together. As they ate and drank, conversation came back to the really horny sex they had all enjoyed. Vince lay there completely enthralled, as Mark and Steven explained to him all about their mutual kink for oil and grease, and how it heightened their lust for each other.

Vince listened excitedly as they then went on to tell him about all the new feelings and sensations they had both experienced, for the first time that day, as a result of wearing their new leather gear against their naked skin. And of course about the really sexy feel of the bike, throbbing between their legs as they drove along, saying how they were both amazed at the animal lust this had brought into their sex.

When they had both finished speaking, Vince laughed as he said, "My arse and mouth can vouch that you were both really turned on tonight! As I told you back in the woods, you both made a dream come true for me. The way you two used me, I was completely out of my head! You're the sexiest young blokes I've ever met!"

They were all laughing, when Vince suddenly exclaimed, "Hey! That reminds me! There are a lot of farms around here, and many of the farm-boys are into motorbikes and wearing leather gear. In fact, I've heard that a group of them have formed a private bikers' club. They have their meetings in an old barn on the Thompson place. One of the guys, Jim, has fucked me a few times. He likes it rough too! But he's not as good as you two!" He laughed again, then went on, "Anyway, Jim told me about the club, and said that if I wanted to go down there he would vouch for me! But the truth is, I didn't have the bottle to go through with it. But maybe if the two of you are interested, the three of us could go together. I know it probably sounds weird, but Id feel much safer letting myself go, if there were a couple of young blokes there that

I knew, rather than just letting a gang of strangers get their hands on me! Even though we were strangers when you stripped me naked and fucked me rotten tonight weren't we? Apparently, Jim told me that things can get pretty wild down there, because like you two, they all get off on the smell and feel of their leathers."

All this talk about horny young farm-hands wearing leather and having hot rampant sex together quickly had its natural effect on all three of them. Looking at each other, they saw their cocks all getting hard again, as their passions rose once more. Nature soon took its course, and in no time at all, the three of them were a tangled mass of arms and legs, their hot, eager young bodies pressed firmly together, as once more, Vince seemed to automatically become the meat in the sandwich, as he whimpered and moaned in ecstasy as Mark and Steven fucked and sucked him without mercy.

At one point during their lusty session, Steven found himself laying on his back on the floor, in a 69 with Vince on top of him. The two of them sucked and slurped greedily on each others rigid cocks, while Mark ploughed Vince's willing and eager arse like there was no tomorrow! And it wasn't until four o'clock in the morning, that they finally dragged their spent and exhausted young bodies up the stairs and into the bathroom once again to wash themselves clean of yet more sweat and sperm. Each of them had shot his load four or five times during that session, and their balls were all drained completely dry.

Feeling very weak, Steven and Mark managed with some effort to pull on their leathers, and at half-past-four, they left the cottage, just as Vince was about to head up to the farmhouse to begin his day's work. But not before it had been arranged that he would speak to Jim, and explain that he had met two randy young men who also wanted to explore their new-found kink for leather. And ask if all three of them would be able to come to the club on the following Friday night. Mark also wrote down their address and phone number, and it was agreed that he would call them on Wednesday night to say if the meeting was on or not. Mark promising Vince, that even if the answer was NO, they would both like to come out and visit him again. And just to add weight to the point, he grabbed Vince's arse and squeezed it hard, while Steven grabbed Vince's cock and did the same!

Vince rolled his eyes in his head as he sighed deeply. Promising faithfully that whatever happened, he would call them on Wednesday night, without fail, from the call-box in the village, swearing on his life that until he saw them again, he wouldn't touch his cock, no matter how hard it got! Then with a parting kiss from each of them, as they squeezed his cock and arse one last time, making Vince tremble and moan with delight, Mark and Steven mounted the bike, fired it into life and set off on the drive home.

Throughout the drive back, Mark kept his arms wrapped around Steven's body and held him tight. There was no doubt in his mind that what had happened with Vince was just hot horny sex! But he knew that he would have to discuss this with Steven, just to make sure that he felt exactly the same way about it. Exploring their kink was one thing, but there was no way that he was going to let it ruin the love they had for each other. So as soon as they had parked the bike in the garage, and Mark had collected the bag with their other clothes in, they let themselves in and made their way quietly up to their room.

Quickly they stripped out of their leathers and jumped into bed together. And as they lay in each others arms under the covers, Mark said, "How do you feel about tonight?" Steven snuggled closer to him before he replied, "What do you mean exactly?" Mark answered, "I mean about us! Having sex with Vince! Wanting to go to this club, where there's sure to be loads of horny sex going on! How do you feel about it?" Steven lifted his head from Marks shoulder and kissed him tenderly, then he said, "If you mean what I think you mean, then as long as it doesn't affect us, affect our love for each other I mean, then it's OK! As long as we don't let it get out of hand." He paused there, and kissed Mark again. Then he laughed as he said, "OK, so were a pair of kinky bastards, with dicks that never go soft! So what! There's nothing wrong in exploring that! Its what we agreed ages ago, isn't it?"

Mark squeezed him tight. Steven continued, "But the only way I want to go ahead with it, is if we are both agreed that it's what we both want. Otherwise, we stick to the oil- bottle and the plastic sheet, and get our kicks that way. And there's always Paul of course. To me, he's like having a gay younger brother. In fact, I love him like a younger brother! And because he respects our relationship, I don't see any harm in us having sex with him. Until he finds a boyfriend of his own that is. Besides, he looks like he's going to turn out just as kinky as we are! What do you say?"

In answer, Mark covered Steven's mouth with his own and kissed him tenderly as he held him close. Then he said, "That's exactly the way that I feel too. Even about Paul. But I just wanted to talk it over with you to make sure that we both felt the same way. We agreed right from the start that we would only do something if it was what we both wanted, and that the only way I want it to be, always." They both fell silent then, and just lay there, stroking each other fondly, neither of them wanting to think that in only a couple of hours they would have to be up to start a new week. And with a final loving and tender kiss, they both drifted off to sleep, Steven having had a birthday weekend he would certainly never forget for the rest of his life.

That Monday was an absolute nightmare for both of them. Having had so little sleep, and with all the rampant sex they had both enjoyed, the day seemed more like three. In fact, they both felt a merciful release when the clock showed that the day was finally over, and they could at last make their weary way home, Steven sure that he had learned nothing, and Mark positive that he had made more mistakes than he wanted to think about. The only thing that either of them wanted to do that evening, was have some food, take a bath together, and flake out in bed and catch up on some sleep.

They were just about to achieve the first of these goals, when there was a gentle knock at the door. Opening it while Mark served up the food, Steven was greeted by the smiling face of Paul, looking disgustingly fit and healthy as always. Steven was just about to say that they were both tired and wanted the evening to themselves, when Paul suddenly threw his arms around his neck and burst out crying uncontrollably.

Managing to close the door, with some difficulty, Steven steered the distraught Paul over to the bed, where they both sat down. Steven looked at Mark who shrugged his shoulders as if to say, Don't look at me! I don't know what's the matter with him! But he did come over and sit on the other side of Paul, putting his arm around him as he said softly, "Tell us what's happened Paul! What's upset you like this?"

Struggling to get control of himself, Paul blurted out, "He's thrown me out! The fucking bastards thrown me out! And all because of a poxy magazine!" Then the sobbing took control again, and his young body heaved in Steven's arms as cried and cried. There was nothing either of them could do but try their best to soothe him, and wait until he was able to get control again. This took some time, and though they both loved him dearly, neither of them could help but look across at their dinner enviously, they were both starving!

But finally Paul cried himself out, and when he noticed their food, which by then was going cold, he couldn't apologise enough, falling over his tongue as he looked from one to the other saying, "Oh shit! I'm sorry! I've spoilt your dinner now! I shouldn't have just come here like that! Oh fuck! I really am sorry! But I didn't know who else to turn to!" Covering Paul's mouth with his hand to silence him, Steven held him tight as he said to Mark, "I don't suppose he's eaten either. Can that be warmed up, and split between the three of us?" Mark smiled at him, then replied, "Probably not! And yes!" So he ruffled Paul's hair as he got up off the bed and went across to the cooker to start re-making dinner. And seeing that Paul was much calmer than before, Steven said to him, "Okay! Now you sit here, or lay down if you want to, while I make us all some coffee! Then you can tell us all about it." And he kissed Paul on the forehead, before getting up himself.

Paul and Steven sat on the bed with two plates of hot food between them, their mugs of coffee on the floor at their feet. Mark sat at the table. As they all devoured the food, Steven said to Paul, "If you're feeling better, tell us what this is all about." Looking up from his plate, Paul glanced sheepishly from one to the other. Then he sighed as he said, "Its so bloody stupid really. All I was doing was lying on my bed naked, in my own room, fisting my dick, and looking at a gay mag I found in some toilets." He needn't have continued, because already Steven and Mark knew what he was going to say next, and could have finished the story for him. But they kept quiet and let him get it out of his system. "Then, before I knew what was happening, he was standing there! My dad! Standing over me! Right beside my bed! He grabbed the magazine out of my hand, threw it across the room, and cracked me across the face with the back of his hand! He was fucking mental! Calling me a filthy pervert and everything else he could think of! And all the time, he just kept hitting me and hitting me! All over! I really thought the bastard was going to kill me!"

They both saw fresh tears welling up in his eyes as he went on, "Then he grabbed me, and dragged me off the bed and started pushing me around, saying that No son of his was going to be a dirty queer!" By then the tears were running down his cheeks again as he went on, "You've never seen my dad! He's a strong bastard! This wasn't the first time he'd ever given me a battering! Anyway, he got the door open and almost picked me up off my feet as he threw me out onto the landing! I just went flying, and landed in a heap at the top of the stairs! Fuck! I was really shitting myself! Then he brought out my clothes, threw them at me, and told me to get them on and get my dirty, queer arse out of his house and never come back! Oh fuck! I've never seen him so mad before! And he stood there, his eyes blazing with hate as I tried to get my clothes on as fast as I could! But even that wasn't fast enough for him, and the next thing I knew, he just lunged for me, got me around the waist, and dragged me down the stairs!"

He looked from one to the other again as he undid the front of his jeans, then he continued, "I was so scared I didn't bother with my boxers. I didn't even have time to do my jeans up! They were still half-way up my legs, and he dragged me along the hall, opened the front door, and threw me out almost naked, onto the street, and slammed the door shut on me! Then while I was crying my eyes out and trying desperately to get my jeans on properly, he opened the front door and threw my trainers and this top at me, then slammed the door shut again. I tell you! I was so fucking scared I didn't know what to do! Then I thought about the only two people who have ever cared about me. So that's when I ran round here!"

For Mark at least, this was no real surprise after the way his own father had acted towards him. Steven on the other hand was completely shocked. And as Paul pulled his top up his body and slipped it off, then slid his jeans down his legs, they both saw some horrific bruises on his body that made their stomachs churn. It was Steven who spoke first, looking at Paul's bruised body and shaking his head from side to side, with tears in his own eyes as he said, "No man should ever be allowed to treat his son like that! He's the one that should be locked up! And he thinks that were the ones that are sick in the head! Well if that's the way so-called normal people behave, then I'm glad I'm fucking queer!" And without even looking at Mark, he went on, "Don't worry Paul. You'll live here with us now. And you'll never have to see that crazy bastard again, if you don't want to."

Mark was in full agreement, and leaving the rest of his meal, he got up, put on his coat and shoes saying, "I'll pop down to the late-chemist and get something to put on those bruises. Get Paul into a warm bath, then when I get back, well put some ointment on him and the three of us will have an early night." And he came over and kissed Steven, then Paul, before he left the room.

The warm water eased some of the pain from Paul's body, and Steven left him in the bath while he washed up. Then he helped him out and being as gentle as he could, dabbed his body dry with a soft bathtowel. They then went back into the room, and Paul lay naked on top of the bed, with Steven beside him, stroking his hair as they talked, and Paul continued to apologise for having caused them both all this trouble.

Steven again assured him that it didn't matter, that he'd done the right thing. And it was just then that Mark came in and Steven said, "Mark! He keeps saying that he shouldn't have brought his troubles to us! Will you tell the silly little bugger he did the right thing! He doesn't seem to believe me!" Mark smiled as he shrugged off his coat, slipped off his shoes and came over to the bed. Kneeling on it, he took a tube of ointment from its box and took off the cap, then as he looked straight into Paul's searching eyes, he smiled broadly and made a fist with his free hand, saying, "Paul! We love you! But you're a stupid bastard, if you think that you can't turn to us when you really need help! Now be told! You are going to live with us now! And when your body is healed, you are going to be, the horny fucking queer-boy that you are! So if you don't want us to smack your arse really hard, just do as you're told! And no more apologising for being in the way! Is that clear?"

Paul groaned, then smiled as he said, "After what you both did to me the other night, you can smack my arse anytime! Oooo! In fact, I know my body's aching like fuck! But if you want to, you can smack my arse right now! Fuck me! That sort of pain really turns me on!" And raising his left hand he stroked Steven's face tenderly as they both watched his cock begin to stir and stiffen as he went on, "And now that you've said that I'm going to live here with you, like I said the other night, I really want you to just strip me naked, smack my bare arse, and squeeze my tits as much as you want to. Honest!" He laughed as he thought of something. Then he looked from one to the other, then down at his dick which was hardening fast, as he said, "In fact, I know my body is really aching from all these bruises. But now that I'm here naked with you, and know I'm safe, even that pains starting to turn me on! I guess I really must be a kinky fucker and no mistake! Would you both like to smack my arse really hard, before you give me a good fucking? So I'll really know what I have to look forward to, now I'm going to be with you all the time!" Once more he searched their faces before adding earnestly, "Please? I really mean it!"

Steven and Mark both stared down in disbelief at Paul's naked and bruised body. HIs solid cock already twitching violently, showing them the sincerity of his words. Suddenly their tiredness was completely forgotten, as they both felt their own cocks rising fast inside their jeans. Hearing no argument, Paul half-turned on his side and pulled Steven's shirt from his waistband and started to unbutton it as he said, "Put the cap back on that ointment Mark, and use it after you've fucked the arse off me!" And as he spread Steven's shirt open wide and started running his warm tongue all over Steven's stomach as his fingers worked to loosen Steven's jeans he said to them both, "And tonight! Please don't be gentle with me because of all the bruises! I really want you to batter the hell out of me! Take a fucking belt to my arse if you want to! I want to find out how much pain I can take! Before it stops turning me on I mean! Will you! Please?"

Again this was something completely new to both of them, although Steven immediately thought back to another Paul in another place, and wondered if this one could have the same level of kink for pain, that the other one did. And as they both stripped out of their clothes, no more was said between them, apart from a warning from Mark who said, "Okay! If that's what you really want, you kinky fucker! But on one condition!" Paul looked at him at once and exclaimed, "Fantastic! What's that?"

Mark replied, "If anything does really hurt you, that you shout stop and well stop immediately! Is that fair?" Paul's face beamed as he replied, "More than fair!" He then went back to licking whatever part of Steven's horny body his tongue could reach. And the instant that Steven and Mark were both naked, they laid into him, using their hands firmly all over his bruised body as they pulled him around and turned him over to expose his sweet round arse-cheeks. Then they both started raining down slaps with the flats of their hands on his vulnerable flesh, until it glowed a deep red. But all they heard from Paul the entire time was a string of satisfied moans and groans as his head spun with lust.

Of his own accord, Paul's mouth found Steven's rigid cock and began sucking on it madly. He worshipped that hard fuck-pole as he gasped repeatedly, "Harder! Harder! Really hurt me! I love it! Oh shit! My dicks so fucking hard, it feels like it's going to burst wide open! Fuck me! This is so wonderful! Get a fucking belt and really lay into my arse as hard as you want, before you fuck me rotten!" It was therefore little wonder that Steven and Mark were soon caught up in the fever of lust, just as they had been the other night, when they'd had Paul naked on their bed.

While Mark went to the wardrobe to get one of his leather belts, Steven leaned right over Paul's slender back, and as Paul greedily sucked and slurped on his solid cock, so Steven reached between Paul's spread legs, grabbed a firm hold on his cock and balls, and pulled them roughly down, so that his raging hard cock was trapped, pointing downwards. Paul loved it. Then Steven pulled and twisted Paul's balls viciously, and he was rewarded with a muffled, "Thank you," from somewhere beneath him.

Returning to the bed with the belt, and having folded it in half, Mark began lashing Paul's glowing arse with it. All this did was to make Paul increase his efforts to suck and slurp on Steven's cock all the more dementedly, as the pain flooded through his horny young body. So from then on, the two of them took it in turns to lash Paul's blistering and red-hot arse-cheeks, while he was allowed to devour the rigid cock of whoever wasn't belting him at the time. Seeing how much he was clearly enjoying this rough treatment, he even got them to use the belt across his back as well. And after he'd taken a really good whipping he still begged them to turn him over and give him more. Laying on his back, his arms stretched out above his head Paul gasped and winced under the searing pain of the lashes that landed across his chest and thighs.

He also gasped his thanks to Steven for the severe torture he was applying to his firm proud nipples. But through it all he stared up at them both with pure love in his eyes and finally he sighed, "Now fuck my arse and mouth with your fabulous hard dicks, and tell me this is how it's always going to be! I want to be your kinky slave-boy from now on! And I want as much pain and fucking as you two want to give me! As well as learning anything else that's really kinky, the two of you want to teach me! I'm all yours now. And I swear I'll never say no to anything you want to do to me! Now fuck me hard, you wonderful, sexy bastards! Fuck my arse and mouth till your hot sperm is running out of me and I pass out!"

Grabbing his swollen shaft in his right fist he squeezed it really hard, making himself gasp loudly. Then he fisted it with all his strength while gazing up at them both, saying in his lust, "My fucking dad was right! I am a filthy pervert!" Stretching his own balls away from his cock with his free hand he gasped with the pain, "And thanks to the two of you, I'm fucking proud of it! Now drag me up onto my hands and knees, and really hammer those stiff dicks into my arse and mouth while you work my tits over again, just like you did before! I love you both! With everything that's in me!"

Two pairs of eager hands grabbed his battered and bruised body and roughly forced him into position, as Mark slid his engorged and throbbing shaft dry into Paul's puckered and twitching fuck-chute, just as he'd been begged to. Meanwhile Steven fed his solid shaft into Paul's hungry mouth and all the way down his throat, as he reached under him and took a firm grip on both his nipples. Paul was then treated to a hard and brutal fucking at both ends as his young body was wracked with pain and flooded with ecstatic pleasure. And while they hammered in and out of his arse and mouth, so Steven and Mark kissed passionately, and Mark whispered, "Perhaps we should introduce him to the oil-bottle? Or even take him to meet Vince? What do you think?"

Panting hard with the delicious sensations Paul's eager mouth sending through his cock, Steven sighed, "Why not! And if he really wants to be our slave, perhaps we should shave those pubes off, and his armpits under his arms as well!" Paul just groaned loudly between them, already out of his head with lust, though all that he'd heard them saying just made his head swim all the more, and he gasped, his entire body shaking, as he grabbed his aching cock just in time to catch his hot sperm and feel it filling his hand. Then he felt Mark firing his hot load right up his arse, while Steven filled his mouth to overflowing.

Seven

By Wednesday evening Paul's body was starting to heal nicely, and when Steven and Mark came home, they were surprised to find that he had not only cleaned and tidied the room, and made the bed, but he had also cooked dinner as well. He was still completely naked, as he'd remained all the time since he arrived on Monday evening, saying that as long as neither of them minded, he felt freer around them. Naturally they didn't mind this at all, although they had refused to have any further heavy sex with him, to allow his young body time to fully heal.

The three of them ate dinner together, after which they were just settling down to watch television when the phone rang. Mark answered it, and was very pleased to hear Vince's voice again. He was even more pleased when Vince told him that he had seen Jim, and that everything was arranged for Friday night, adding hopefully, "If the two of you are still interested?" Then he thanked them both again for the wonderful sex they had all enjoyed, assuring Mark that whenever they felt like repeating it, he would be more than willing. Covering the mouthpiece Mark whispered to Steven, "Well! Do we go on Friday night, or not? And do I tell Vince about Paul, or keep him as a surprise!" Paul's mouth dropped open as he listened to this, but he said nothing, as Steven smiled at Mark and nodded his consent, saying, "But lets keep Paul our secret! At least until we see how he feels about it all!"

Mark then confirmed that they would meet Vince at his cottage at 7-30 pm, and the three of them would go on from there. But no sooner had Mark put down the receiver, than unable to contain his curiosity another second, Paul said, "What's happening on Friday night that you want to see how I feel about?" Smiling at Steven, Mark said, "He's a nosy little bastard, this one, isn't he?" Steven laughed, then proceeded to explain to Paul all about how they had come to meet Vince in the woods, and how he had told them about the bikers' club, and said he would try and fix it for them to go there with him, for some really hot action.

Paul's eyes were open wide with amazement, as was his mouth. He exclaimed, "Wow! That sounds really wicked! Do you think this Vince would let me come as well?" Then he paused and looked down, saying quietly, "That is, if the two of you want to take me of course. If not, I can just stay here, while you go off and enjoy yourselves." Mark and Steven looked at each other, then back at Paul. Then Mark said, "These young blokes are all into leather, and other kinky stuff! Some of them will probably like their sex rough! Are you sure you're ready for that? Doing it with us is one thing, but with complete strangers? It could get pretty heavy you know!" Lifting his head again Paul looked at them both, and saw the genuine concern on their faces. Then he replied, "But you two would still be there! So Id still be kind of safe, wouldn't I?"

Steven and Mark were both silent, unable to find an answer to that one. So Paul went on, "Anyway, I'm still waiting to find out what you two meant about showing me the oil-bottle and shaving my pubes off. Has that all got something to do with this?" Both of them had forgotten about that, but clearly Paul hadn't. So once again Steven explained to Paul all about their mutual kink for being covered in oil, and how it affected them both. Finishing off by saying, "And as for shaving you, well that was just a joke, said when we were both really horny!"

But Paul had cottoned onto a new idea and he wasn't about to let go of it that easily. And he was already stroking his cock as he said, "Well, if these young blokes want a naked slaves body to do anything they want to, why don't you show me what it's like? You know from the other night that I really get turned-on by rough sex, and having my body whipped and everything! So why don't the pair of you tie me to the bed, then shave all the hair off my body! Then you can show me what you mean about the oil! And I can see if it does anything for me too!"

The trouble with Paul was, that for Steven and Mark he was just too sexy. Either of them only had to look at his beautiful naked body for more than five minutes, and they automatically started feeling horny. And watching him sitting there, stroking his already solid and delicious cock while he turned-on to the idea of having his body shave didn't leave them any option but to agree.

Being inventive, they stripped the long laces out of their trainers to tie Paul's wrists and ankles to the four corners of the bed, though not as tightly as he wanted them to, for fear of cutting off his circulation. Then once he was spread-eagled, they slowly stripped naked while he watched, and saw his cock bouncing up and down wildly in anticipation of what was to come.

Mark then brought their two razors and some shaving foam from the bathroom, along with some towels. The first thing they did was to lift Paul's body up off the bed while they worked a bathtowel under him to save any water soaking their bedclothes. This done, they both worked shaving foam all over his pubes until they had a good lather and Paul was moaning with pleasure at their touch. Then Steven poured some hot water into a plastic bowl and brought this over to the bed, so that they could dip the razors in it and keep them clean as they shaved him.

Finally the moment arrived. They both picked up their razors and deliberately showed them to him, holding them close to his face as Steven said, "Say good-bye to that nice bush of manly hair you have over your cock Paul! When we've finished, you'll be as smooth down there as everywhere else on your boy-body!"

In response, Paul's rigid cock slapped madly against his stomach, the exposed head becoming covered in lather, as he moaned, "Oh yes! Shave off my pubes! Then I'll really look like a slave won't I? Fuck! This feels so kinky! Being tied up completely helpless and having you shave my body! Wow! What a turn-on! Do it to me! Do it now before I shoot my load just thinking about it!" And both of them took a firm hold of his aching shaft, driving him wild with lust as their hands bent his cock downwards and held it there throbbing like crazy as they started to shave off his full bush of pubic hair.

Noticing as they did so, that not only did Paul gaze down constantly at their own throbbing hard cocks, but also at their own pubes that crowned them. But before long there wasn't one single hair left and his cock appeared almost to have doubled in size at their absence. It was then time for them to turn their attention to his armpits, and this they did more speedily, lathering them both and taking one each, so that in seconds they too were shaved completely smooth also. Then Steven washed Paul's crotch and armpits, while Mark dried them with the towel, before they both stood back to admire their handywork, noting that Paul them looked even sexier than before, if that were ever possible.

As a reward, they both then climbed back onto the bed and knelt beside him. Leaning forward against the headboard, they both brushed their swollen cocks across his parted lips. They teased him with them like that for several minutes, then allowed him to move his hungry mouth from one to the other, sucking dementedly, and wiping their saliva-coated cocks all over his face until he was begging to be untied and fucked in his favourite position. But after making him suffer this torment for a while longer, they both climbed off the bed leaving Paul looking very bewildered. Then they quickly pulled out the plastic sheet, the large can of oil, and the oil-bottle.

Paul watched their every movement in fascination, firing a stream of questions at them, all of which they ignored, as they worked together to clear the floor-space and spread the large sheet of black plastic over the carpet. Only when they had filled the oil-bottle and everything was ready, did they approach the bed again, closing in on him. Without speaking they quickly untied his bonds, and with Mark grabbing Paul's wrists and Steven his ankles, they carried him off the bed and laid him down in the middle of the sheeting, once more spreading his arms and legs wide and ordering him to keep them that way.

Paul's engorged cock slapped wildly against his stomach and his eyes were wide with curiosity as Steven picked up the oil-bottle. He lay perfectly still as Steven then started at his throat, and squeezed out a steady stream of the clear-brown liquid all the way down his body to his crotch. He then did the same down each leg and finally along each arm. After this, Steven put the bottle down and the two of them began spreading the oil all over Paul's prone body with their hands.

This had him moaning and sighing almost instantly, and they were both delighted when they saw that the feel and smell of the slippery oil covering his horny young body was clearly having the effect on Paul they had hoped for. Steven then held his hand to Paul's nose and told him to breath in deeply, and while he did this, Mark poured more oil all over Paul's painfully hard cock and full balls, then began massaging the oil into them with both hands. The effect was electric. Instantly Paul's chest and stomach began heaving as he gasped and panted, his eyes glazed over and his mind became totally sex-crazed. As he writhed around on the sheet, his cock throbbing so hard and his arse twitching so badly he was almost crying with frustration as he yelled, "Shit! This is so fucking kinky! Why didn't you do this to me before! I'm so fucking horny I feel like my heads going to explode! Oh yeah! Give me more of this! And hurry up and ram your dicks in me too! Before I go completely mental!"

This was more than Steven and Mark could have hoped for. Excitedly they pounced on Paul and turned him onto his stomach. Then covered the whole of his back with oil in the same way, making sure that they both worked the oil all over his arse-cheeks and down inside his arse-crack. Paul was squirming around under their hands, gasping and moaning and begging to be fucked. But they still had to cover each other with oil, so they turned him over again, spreading his arms and legs wide once more. And to make sure that he stayed as sex-crazed as he was, they then knelt on either side of his heaving body, Steven trapping Paul's left arm under his right leg and Mark trapping his right arm under his left leg.

This meant that Paul had to watch in mind-blowing agony, as the two people he loved most in the entire world sprayed oil over each others sexy young bodies and throbbing hard cocks, then spread it all over each other, right above him, while all he could do was watch them; his lust driving him completely insane. Never in his life before had anything turned him on so powerfully. He pleaded and whimpered and begged in every way he could think of to get them to stop this sadistic torture, and fuck his mouth and arse until he couldn't take any more, leaving Steven and Mark in no doubt at all, that their young sexy friend was indeed even kinkier than they were.

But once the oil had its effect on their senses as well, they were also certain that this was not all just for Paul's benefit. They also wanted to enjoy themselves too. So releasing Paul's arms they both lay down with his hot horny body trapped between their own. Then they began running their hands all over him, while all three of them kissed each other passionately and Marks solid cock slipped up and down in Paul's arse-crack as they worked their slippery bodies repeatedly against each other, driving them all wild with lust. In fact they kept up this nightmare of lust and passion until Paul gasped and gasped, as his long-engorged cock fired off a stream of thick white spunk between his and Steven's body, though he had been unable to get his hand anywhere near it.

Paul was so out of his head with lust by then, that his cock stayed just as solid, just as painfully hard, as Steven kept sliding against him spreading the warm sperm over their bodies until Paul was nearly in tears with frustration as he pleaded his life away just to feel their fabulous hard dicks hammering in and out of his two screaming fuck-holes. That was the moment they decided to have mercy on him, and before he knew it he had been mauled and dragged up onto his hands and knees. Then Steven stretched under the bed and brought out a new tin of axle-grease.

Taking the lid off, he deliberately held the tin under Paul's nose and laughed as he watched Paul nearly pass out as the strong smell filled his nose. He then dipped his fingers into the gooey black mess and pulled out a large sticky dollop. Smiling at Paul and kissing him before he said, "This is going up your arse, you sexy fucker!" Paul's eyes rolled in his head as Steven slithered his way down Paul's body where Mark was already in position between his wide-spread legs, stroking his solid cock. Wasting no more time, Steven slapped the thick black treacle straight on Paul's desperately puckered hole and started working it into his arse. Paul groaned deeply and his entire body trembled as Steven slid one, then two, then three fingers, deep inside his arse.

And the instant that he felt these pull out of him to be replaced immediately by Marks solid cock-head, as it slipped smoothly past his sphincter, he gasped and shot as his cock fired off a second powerful load of hot sperm all over the sheet under him. But his moans of ecstasy were quickly muffled as Mark slid his shaft all the way inside his arse and Steven slid his rigid cock into Paul's open mouth and right down his throat.

His mind still reeling under the impact of his orgasm, his body impaled on two beautiful throbbing hard cocks, Paul was then trapped in the position he had come to love the most. And as Steven and Mark began working their rampant cocks in and out of his two fuck-holes, he groaned in demented agony as somewhere in his brain he also realised that even then, his own dick was throbbing just as wildly, just as painfully hard between his spread legs.

That session more than satiated their lust for the next two days. But by Friday evening their hormones were working overtime again as they anticipated the hot and horny sex that they hoped waited for them out in the country. Naturally Paul had spent the last two days bombarding them both with an endless stream of questions about Vince. How sexy was he? Was he kinky too? What did they know about the other farm-boys? So to shut him up they had told him about Vince's kink for dressing up in a police uniform in the woods, and walking around wearing it and turning himself on. And about the times he had caught two young men naked, having sex together, and how he had used the uniform to get them both to service his cock and arse as well.

Paul thought that was really kinky and said that he certainly couldn't wait to meet Vince, and the other horny boys in their leather gear. Steven and Mark had of course planned to drive out there on the bike, but that would have meant a real problem in getting Paul there as well. He did say that he could borrow a push-bike from one of his mates, as long as they didn't drive too fast. But that didn't seem really fair to them, so Mark spoke to a new friend of his at work, and announced on Thursday night that his friend had agreed to lend him his car for the weekend. This news was greeted with great cheers from both Paul and Steven.

Arriving home on Friday, Steven and Mark were greeted by a bubbling and excited Paul. He'd already done all the cleaning during the day, had had his own bath, and had cooked dinner for them all. They were also both pleased and surprised to see their leathers laid out neatly on the bed. Quickly they all wolfed down their meal, then while Steven and Mark stripped off and went into the bathroom to have a bath, Paul washed the dishes and put everything away neatly. And when the other two came back into the room still drying themselves, they found Paul on his knees rummaging about in a large plastic sack. He looked up when they entered the room and smiled saying, "I went round to my house this afternoon, when I knew my mum would be home alone. She gave me the same shit that my dad did, but at least she let me in, and gave me this sack to stuff my clothes in."

Then he pulled out a pair of old, ripped jeans and a shirt that had been spattered with paint. Holding these up for Steven and Mark to see he said, "If I wear these tonight, then it won't matter how rough things get! What do you think?" Sliding into his leather trousers, Steven said, "Put them on and lets have a look at you!" So Paul quickly pulled on his old jeans, leaving them open, slipped on the shirt, and tucked it inside his jeans before doing them up.

Coming to stand in front of them both, Paul smiled as he asked nervously, "Do they make me look like I'm ready for anything?" Looking him up and down as they both walked around him, Mark said, "Not quite!" And quickly getting a sharp knife from the cabinet drawer, he hooked the tip of the blade into a small hole he had seen just at the bottom of Paul's right arse-cheek. They all heard the material rip as Mark cut a slash about four inches long across the leg of Paul's jeans, so that when the knife was removed the smooth curving flesh of his arse-cheek could be clearly seen. Steven then took the knife from him, and did the same to a hole on Paul's thigh only about an inch below where his cock was hanging down his left leg.

Taking out the knife, Steven then demonstrated that he could then slide his hand inside the slit straight onto Paul's cock, while Mark did the same with the slit he'd made and Paul felt his warm hand caressing his right arse-cheek. Paul just stood there and sighed happily. Then Steven used the knife again to cut off most of the buttons from Paul's shirt leaving his smooth chest fully exposed. Telling Paul to then go and look at himself in the mirror in the wardrobe, Steven and Mark finished dressing. And once an even more excited Paul had slipped an old pair of trainers on his feet, they all left the room and went downstairs, sure that they were all going to have the time of their lives that night.

They arrived outside Vince's cottage dead on time, and he immediately opened the door and greeted them warmly. His eyes particularly lit up when he saw Paul. He too was wearing leathers, but not new like theirs. He wore a worn leather jacket, worn, tight leather trousers, and an old pair of leather boots. The three of them were already quite horny from their drive. Not least because Paul had discovered that as soon as he sat down in the back seat of the car, his cock poked out of the slit in the leg of his jeans.

Naturally he couldn't keep his hands off it, and it quickly became hard as his mind flooded with all sorts of sexy ideas, which he talked about constantly. Therefore, it was a big temptation to get Vince and Paul stripped naked, and start the fun and games early as they all kissed and embraced each other. Paul finding that Vince's hands which automatically went to his arse as they kissed, found the slit and his left hand slipped inside to get his first feel of Paul's naked flesh, something that Paul had absolutely no objection to at all, as at first sight he'd thought how sexy Vince looked. But prizing Paul and Vince apart, Steven and Mark pointed out that they didn't want to spoil the fun they were all looking forward to, so reluctantly they all kept themselves in check and got into the car for the drive to the Thompson place. Vince sitting in the back with Paul, his right slipping between Paul's spread legs to stroke his already throbbing cock as he gave Mark directions.

Arriving at the barn, Paul was already turned-on like crazy and sporting a solid throbbing bulge in the front of his jeans, making the slit across his thigh open wide, showing his smooth soft flesh beneath. Hearing the car pull up, Jim came out to meet them. He was tall and slim and Vince had already told them that he was just eighteen. He was dressed in full leathers like everyone else, except Paul. Vince introduced them all, and as they shook hands Jim laughed as he looked behind them at the car saying, "Vince said you had a new Honda!" Mark smiled as he replied, "We have! But we didn't know we'd be bringing Paul with us. So I had to borrow the car from a friend at work."

Mark noticing that Jim was surveying each of their crotches with an eagle eye while he listened to what he was saying. This sent a shiver of excitement coursing through all of them, and they were wondering already what Jim would look like stripped out of his leathers. He led them all inside the barn; at first glance it appeared much as they expected. That was until they all noticed that the floor of one of the stalls was completely covered with black plastic sheeting. And they spotted the large cans of axle-grease and engine oil stacked up against the wooden partition. Then they saw the many thick, woollen blankets, laid out across bales of hay in several of the other stalls. Instantly they all felt their cocks stiffening fast. Steven and Marks attention was naturally already on the oil and the plastic sheets.

Once again, Paul felt Vince's hand slip inside the slit in the back of his jeans and onto his arse, while Jim slid his hand into the other slit, and began fondling Paul's already rigid and aching cock. All four of the visitors were certain already that they were in for a really good night of hot horny lust. Inside the barn, there were already six other farm-boys sitting on some bales in one of the stalls. Reluctantly taking his hand off Paul's rigid cock, Jim took them over and introduced them. "Steven, Mark, Paul. This is John. He's just had his eighteenth birthday two weeks ago, and since his initiation, he's now our youngest member. But he's got a dick on him that just doesn't know the meaning of soft!"

John smiled at them all as he got up from the bale he was sitting on. Stepping closer to them all, he pulled open the front of his skin-tight jeans, letting a solid throbbing eight inch cock spring out for them all to see, that was easily as fat as any of their wrists. As he stroked it with his left hand, with his right he reached out and unashamedly groped each of their crotch-es, squeezing their own solid cocks as he nodded approvingly. With a quick prompt from Jim they then all followed suit, and squeezed his beau-tiful hard dick one after the other, then leaving his jeans wide open, John went and sat down again, still stroking his solid rod. The next member that Jim introduced them to was Dave. Jim told them that he was twenty, and just looking at him they could see them that he was well-built, with a pow-erful, muscular body.

Dave then got to his feet and came to stand in front of them all, as he did the same as John, pulling his jeans open wide to flop out a solid, heav-ily-veined nine-inch dick that made Steven and Paul's mouths drool instantly. After Dave had groped them all, and as they did the same to him, Jim informed them that most of all, Dave liked to fuck until he dropped.

Paul in particular felt his knees go weak as he stared at Dave's fantastic weapon. And he smiled at Dave as he said weakly, "You can shove that up my arse anytime!" Dave winked at him, then turned and went back to sit with the others.

They were then introduced to Danny, and Jim told them that he was twenty-five, and the oldest member of the club. Danny opened his leather jacket then spread the front of his leather trousers wide, showing them that just like all of the others, he was wearing nothing under them. They could all see how really skinny he was, but Steven and Mark paid very close attention to him, as Jim informed them all that it was Danny and John who were most into using the oil and grease as part of their hot and horny sex. Danny was stroking a solid seven inch cock, which Steven and Mark squeezed quite hard when it came to their turn to grope him. And Steven said to him, "Mark and I like oil very much too!" Danny's eyes lit up at this news, and he replied, "Well look forward to seeing you naked, over in the stall then!" Steven gave Danny's balls a squeeze making him gasp as he said, "You bet," as he winked at him.

After Danny sat down again, Phil was the next to be introduced. Jim informed them that he was nineteen. Standing up, he first pulled down the zip on his leather jacket opening it wide, then he came towards them undoing his leather trousers as he walked. They all saw that he had a slender, swimmer's body, with skin as smooth as silk, noticing that he had the most sexy green eyes, that made them all go weak at the knees. He also flopped out a solid seven-inch cock as well, and stood stroking it proudly for their inspection.

Then came Tony. Jim told them that he was twenty, and that he and Phil were boyfriends. Though he went on to say that they both lived on separate farms, and that although they used the club to meet each other, they still liked to have open sex with the rest. Tony's dick was only six inches long, but nonetheless desirable. But no-one was at all surprised to hear that he liked getting fucked by as many cocks as wanted to slide up his tight little arse.

The last member to be introduced was called Simon. Jim told them that he was nearly nineteen, and just like John, always had a hard-on and was ready for anything. Simon was quite short, only 5 6" tall. He had thick blond hair, a boyish face, and unlike the rest, as he came towards them he stripped out of his clothes completely, to stand naked, his legs spread wide apart and with his hands locked behind his head then turned around slowly giving them all a good look at his slender smooth body and solid eight inch cock that stood straight up his stomach and throbbed wildly.

He didn't grope them, but they certainly needed no encouragement to run their hands all over his hot naked young body, hearing him moan softly at their touches as they surrounded him; four pairs of hands caressing him everywhere. The sight of so many beautiful, horny young men, all of them aching to get naked and into some really hot action was just incredible. Glancing around, Steven and Mark saw that Vince already had Paul stripped naked. They also saw the admiring glances from Jim and the others, as they saw that Paul's slender body was completely shaven, as Vince dropped down on his knees, his leather trousers open wide, as he began sucking and slurping on Paul's solid cock.

But after only a few seconds, Jim pulled Vince roughly to his feet, leading him and Paul both away to one of the other stalls. With Simon then on his knees in front of them, his hands still locked behind his head, his mouth already drooling with lust as his eyes passed from one bulging crotch to another, they saw Dave going over to join Vince and the others, no doubt drawn by Paul's open offer of his fresh willing arse. After what they had been told, it seemed perfectly natural to see that Phil and Tony had gone into yet another of the stalls, where Phil was quickly stripping Tony and kissing him passionately. And finally, what Steven and Mark had both most been waiting for: there on the plastic sheeting stood John and Danny, shedding their clothes to reveal hot, horny young bodies, ready and eager for some real action!

Looking down at Simon, Mark nodded towards the stall where John and Danny stood, their bodies pressed close together, their hands caressing each others bodies dementedly, while they kissed deeply and desperately. He said, "You into that too?" Instantly Simon replied, "I'm into whatever you two horny young blokes want to do to me! Just ask any of them! You don't need to ask me anything! Just take me, and do whatever you want to me! That's what I like most, and it turns me on like fuck!" He glanced at Paul, already secured in lined, leather wrist and ankle cuffs, seeing him fully spread-eagled, with Dave's well-built body in between his spread legs, hammering his nine-inch arse-stretcher in and out of Paul's fuck-hole. Jim's solid eight-inch cock was buried deep down Paul's throat, and Vince was busy moving backwards and forwards between sucking on Paul's firm, proud nipples and sucking on his throbbing hard cock.

Eight

Satisfied that Paul was clearly in good hands, they both grabbed Simon roughly by his upper arms and dragged his naked body across the floor, over to John and Danny, who were really getting into each other. But they separated, smiling delightedly, when Simon, who they already knew was the willing and eager club-slave, was dragged into the stall, then thrown down on the black plastic at their feet. Steven and Mark then stood right over Simon as they quickly stripped out of their leathers, getting a willing hand from John and Danny, who ran their hands all over their hot young bodies, feeling the smooth softness of their naked flesh, feeling their lust surging inside them, making them want to have mind-blowing, horny sex with these two young men, as each of them sucked avidly on their sweet rosebud nipples, making them stand out firm and proud.

Once they were all naked, one of the large oil cans was opened by John. Lying completely still, Simon kept his arms and legs spread wide, his chest already rising and falling with lust, as oil was poured all over the front of his horny young body. Getting down on their knees around him, the four men ran their hands all over him, spreading the oil everywhere, and driving Simon wild with lust. After that, they turned him over onto his stomach and did the same all over his back and the back of his legs and arms, John and Mark paying very careful attention to Simon's sweet, high, rounded arse-cheeks which they moulded lovingly with their hands, before spreading them wide to oil his already twitching fuck-hole, feeling him squirm beneath them.

This done, they left Simon moaning and writhing around on the sheeting, clenching and releasing his arse-cheeks, his lust in full control, as he ground his rigid cock against the slippery sheeting, his eyes glazed. But they left him to suffer his demented sex-lust while they took it in turns covering each others sexy, horny young bodies with oil too, each of them enjoying to the limit, having a new, supple, smooth naked body to run their hands all over. In fact, they all delighted in each others horny nakedness as well as the feel and smell of the oil covering their warm young bodies, driving them so crazy with lust, that Simon was almost screaming with desperation for them to drive their rigid, wonderful dicks deep inside his two desperately yearning fuck-holes.

Tears of frustration flooded from his eyes as he turned over again and watched Danny and Steven get down into a slippery 69, their painfully hard cocks being the only part of them not to have oil on them, as they had both agreed. But the next second, his fuck-hole was twitching violently again, as John came and knelt down with his beautiful silken-soft thighs spread wide on either side of Simon's head, making him tilt his head backwards. Instantly Simon's eyes were locked onto John's iron-hard, throbbing cock bouncing around with almost a mind of its own, only inches above his face.

Automatically Simon opened his mouth wide, and ran his wet tongue around his lips, as he groaned and panted, his nipples standing out proud from his heaving chest as he was filled with a desperately longing to get that fantastic, thick-shafted eight-inch cock buried all the way down his cock-hungry throat, yet not daring to touch it, until he was allowed to do so, which made his torment even worse, staring at it bouncing around and sending him insane with lust, and not caring in the least that it was all shiny and covered in oil. He hadn't even realised that Mark was kneeling between his widespread legs until he felt him grasp his ankles and start to fold his legs back so that his knees soon met and pressed against his chest, leaving his fuck-hole fully exposed.

Gasping and panting heavily he screamed, "Oh fuck me! Fuck me! Please! Oh shit! I want it so bad! Oh p-l-e-a-s-e! P-l-e-a-s-e! F-u-c-k M-eee!" Mark then told John to hold Simon's ankles and pull his legs right back so that his arse was lifted high off the sheeting. Mark was very pleased with this, because it made it easier for him to slap a large dollop of black sticky axle-grease right on Simon's exposed fuck-hole, John insisting that Mark take first poke at Simon's sweet man-cunt. Mark sighed deeply, as he found just how good Simon's arse-chute felt on his aching shaft, as he slid right into him smoothly. Then pressing down on the backs of Simon's legs he began fucking him immediately.

Seeing this, Danny and Steven split up and came over to join in the fun. Simon was both pleased and surprised when Danny lifted his head from between John's legs and fed his own solid cock right down his throat. At the same time, Steven ran his hands all over John's soft and sexy young body, kissing him passionately, and playing with his nipples, while keeping his cock rigid and throbbing wildly as he waited for his turn in Simon's arse.

To all of them, Simon looked even more sexy with his legs spread wide and folded back against his chest, getting his arse well and truly fucked repeatedly by John and Marks two wonderfully hard cocks, while his mouth slurped hungrily on Danny and Steven's deliciously warm hard fuck-poles. It was no surprise to anyone, that with all of this hot attention, Simon soon shot his own full load of thick white spunk all over his sweat-soaked, oil-slicked young body without having touched his cock once. But then he wrapped his right fist around the still-hard and throbbing shaft and kept pumping it furiously, and being so turned-on, as they continued to fuck the hell out of him, he fired another three hot loads, one after the other, over his sexy young body. All five of them were fully and completely absorbed in each other, and the pure lust that filled the air around them.

And while this passionate exchange of lust was going on in the oil enclosure, over in the first stall, Jim had released Paul and secured Vince in the wrist and ankle cuffs, leaving a well-fucked Paul, his dick still desperately hard, his mind swimming with lust, to stagger over to the stall where Phil was busy fucking Tony with all his pent-up desire. It was then Vince's turn to get his arse plugged by Jim's solid aching cock, while Dave fed his nine-inch fuck-rod in and out of Vince's cock-hungry mouth, both of them making sure that Vince didn't touch his own solid dick, to keep his lust fully on the boil.

Seeing a glazed-eyed Paul stagger into their stall, his rampant cock leading the way, Phil at once slid his dick out of Tony's arse, both of them being more than happy to get their hands on Paul's slender, hot young body. They laid him down on the blankets that covered the hay bales, while they both treated him to a mind-blowing tongue-bath. In only a few seconds Paul was once more out of his mind with lust and desperately wanting to get fucked again. Phil was certainly happy to oblige their new visitor, so quickly turned Paul onto his stomach, spread his legs wide, and slid his solid cock right up him on the copious sperm that was oozing out of his still half-open fuck-hole. Paul gasped in ecstasy as he felt yet another wonderful cock starting to fuck his brains out. But Tony quickly silenced him, by feeding him his rigid cock, which Paul instantly took right into his mouth and began sucking and slurping on greedily, knowing for certain that he was already having the time of his life.

Glancing over the top of the stalls, Dave's eyes spotted Danny. There was something about Danny's desperately thin, body that turned him on like nothing else. He also had no aversion to being covered in oil himself, as part of his life on the farm, working on the farm machinery, the same as the rest of them. So sliding his solid cock out of Vince's eager mouth, he got up and strode over to the oil-enclosure. Walking up to where Danny was fucking Simon's mouth, Dave bent down, wrapped his strong young arms around Danny's body, and picked him up and carried him off, back to the stall where Jim was hammering his cock in and out of Vince. It was easy to see that Danny was also heavily attracted to Dave, because as he was being carried across the barn, he reached up, wrapped his hands behind Dave's head, and while feeling Dave's rigid fuck-rod between his legs, twisted his head and kissed him desperately.

Arriving back in the stall, Dave told Jim to pull out of Vince and stand back. Seeing Dave holding Danny in his arms, Jim slid his cock out of Vince's arse and stood aside. Dave then laid Danny face-down on top of Vince's sweat-drenched young body, and Danny started kissing Vince passionately, Dave winked at Jim as he said, "Two holes are always better than one!" And he quickly worked Danny's willing body into position, so that his and Vince's holes were directly above each other. Then he slid deep inside Danny's arse and began fucking him, before pulling right out and sliding smoothly up Vince's fuck-chute.

Jim liked this idea as well, and he went around to the other end of the two horny young men, where he was quickly doing the same, tilting back Vince's head to feed his solid cock right down his throat, then after a few seconds sliding it out only to slide it immediately into Danny's equally hungry mouth. Back in the oil-stall, Steven and Mark had been very happy to see that both Danny and John as well as Simon, got turned on by the smell and feel of the oil on their sexy young bodies just as much as they did. The temperature was rising rapidly, and after Simon had two loads of hot sperm shot up inside his arse, and one down his throat, he was allowed to get up.

Steven then took his place, and immediately John got between his legs, lifting them high as he buried his solid shaft all the way inside him. Steven sighed deeply, having waited so long to feel one of these solid cocks up his twitching arse. While Mark fucked Steven's mouth and played with his firm proud nipples, Simon was told to lick out both of their arses, while keeping his hands well away from his own aching hard cock. Simon worked between John and Mark licking and lapping at their sweet young arses, while running his hands all over their hot sweating bodies as they fucked Steven into oblivion.

Changing places after a while, John and Mark decided to let Steven have a different cock in his two more-than-eager holes. John then leaned forward over Steven's body, still keeping his cock buried in Steven's hungry throat. Sliding his warm wet mouth all the way down Steven's rigid pole, he sucked and slurped on it, while thrusting his young hips backwards and forwards, fucking Steven's slobbering mouth.

This then allowed Steven to see something he had never seen before, as he lay on his back, being fucked, sucked, and with a dick down his own throat, so he looked up at John's ball-sack dangling over his head and watched Simon hungrily eating out John's arse as if it were the most exquisite delicacy imaginable. This had to be without any doubt, the hottest, horniest sex Steven had even experienced, and his lust instantly went into overdrive. And it was only ten minutes later that three newcomers slipped silently into the sex-filled atmosphere.

They stood just inside the door, surveying the scene of naked lust, as their cocks sprang instantly to throbbing hardness inside their jeans, and their heads began to spin with desire. Desperately shedding their clothes, Jim spotted the newcomers and slid his cock out of Danny's mouth and came over to welcome them. Hugging and kissing each of them, he told them about the three new guests that had joined them for the evening.

Bringing the three new horny members across to the oil-stall to introduce them, Jim said, "Steven, Mark, this is Carl, Michael and Barry." He groped the crotch of each horny naked young man as he introduced him, while Steven and Mark looked them up and down, feeling their lust soaring to even new heights. Jim went on, "Carl is twenty-one, and just like Paul and Simon he has an always ready mouth and arse!" He squeezed Carls arse as he said this, and Carl opened his mouth and ran his tongue around his lips as his cock jerked violently. He then pushed Carl forward, straight into the arms of John who had stood up when they came over.

Folding his arms around Carls naked body John kissed him, working his oil-covered hands and body against Carls smooth clean flesh. Carl moaned softly, and Steven reached up, sliding his own oil-covered left hand up and down the back of Carls legs and caressing his firm arse-cheeks smearing them with oil too. Simon at once got on his knees behind Carl, spreading his arse-cheeks wide to bury his face right in his arse-crack and start licking and lapping at his fuck-hole. Mark had stopped fucking Steven, slid his cock out of his lovers arse and got up, standing with his rigid cock on full display for the other newcomers to see.

Slipping his arms around both of their waists, Jim hugged them tightly as he smiled saying, "Michael here, is twenty-two, and he loves having Simon lick out his arse for a long time, before he rewards him with a good hard fucking! While Barry, who's nineteen, well, he just loves to have sex!" Michael and Barry stepped up and put their arms around Mark kissing him in turn as they felt his body all over, while he did the same to them.

Jim then led Michael and Barry away to the other stalls. And while Mark turned his attention to Carls horny young body, along with Steven and John, who were already getting him well-oiled and as high as they were. Michael and Barry both joined Phil and Tony and were introduced to Paul, who was more than happy to see yet more naked and horny young men, their dicks raging hard and ready to play with him.

So it went on, until they had moved out of their stalls onto the floor of the barn in an orgy. Every arse that craved a good stiff cock was fucked and filled repeatedly with hot sperm. Those who enjoyed the added thrill of pain, with their arses and backs well beaten, their nipples twisted, bitten and bruised. Every mouth that loved sliding up and down on a solid shaft guzzled down load after load of delicious creamy sperm, moaning delightedly. Until well into the early hours of the morning, they all lay sprawled out around the barn, their balls drained, their young bodies all covered in oil and axle-grease and completely exhausted. But when everyone's lust was finally satiated, it was Marks arms that Steven dragged his well-fucked, sperm and oil-covered body into. Steven's arse had been fucked by almost every cock in the barn, while Mark had fucked all the smooth round arses he could till his balls were empty.

As they lay there amidst all those beautiful naked young bodies, gazing deeply into each others eyes, both knew that without question they would look forward to Jim inviting them to come back to the club again and again. Never in their lives had they experienced such sexual freedom, with so many beautiful, horny young men determined to enjoy sex, and their sexuality to the limit!

But equally, there was no doubt, that fantastic as all the mind-blowing sex had been, their love for each other was just as strong as ever. Kissing and holding each other tenderly, they both glanced across at Paul and smiled at each other, happy to see him laying in Vince's arms, and staring deeply into his eyes as they talked quietly together, seeming for all the world to be as much in love with each other, as they were.

Slowly the young men started to get up and walk over to another corner of the barn, where there were two large urns, full of hot water. There were also several large canisters containing cold water. Working in pairs, they all cleaned themselves up, getting the worst of the oil, grease and dried sperm from each other using plenty of industrial-strength detergent which they brought from their farms. After this, they all dressed, their young bodies still dripping wet, and with final hugs and kisses, they started to leave.

But before they left, Jim came over to Steven and the others and said, "All the members agree that the three of you were fantastic sex! So I've been asked to tell you, that you're all welcome to come back and join us any time you want to!" He beamed a broad smile at them all, cupping Paul's left arse-cheek in his hand and giving it a squeeze. Then he went on, "In fact, we'd like to make all three of you honourary members of the club! Even though you're not farm-boys like us, you're the hottest, horniest sex any of us has ever had, apart from between ourselves of course!"

Then to Paul he whispered, "And you're welcome to strip naked for me, anytime, you sexy fucker!" Thanking him for the invitation, they all assured him that they would indeed come again and again, to enjoy many more hot and raunchy orgies, with so many sex-crazed and eager young men, who had ideas so similar to their own. Then the four of them left the barn and climbed wearily into the car and drove off, heading for Vince's cottage. During the drive it came as very little surprise to either Steven or Mark when Paul announced, "When we get to Vince's place, I won't be coming back with you! We both got on so we'll together back there in the barn, that he's asked me to come and live on the farm with him. And today he's going to ask the farmer if hell give a job on farm! Apparently he said to Vince only a couple of days ago, that he was thinking about taking somebody else on! And Vince doesn't think there'll be any problem about us living together in his cottage!"

Steven and Mark both told him how happy they were that the two of them wanted to be together. And Mark said that they would bring his clothes out for him that evening, once they'd had some sleep. So when they reached the cottage, instead of going inside with Vince and Paul, they all kissed and hugged each other, and Paul whispered in Steven's ear, "You and Mark can still give my arse and mouth a good fucking when you come out to go to the barn you know! I think I'm really going to be happy living out here with Vince. But my body will still be yours, whenever you want it, and I'll make sure and tell Vince that, because without the two of you, Id never have found out what a horny sex-machine I really am!"

Steven hugged him tight and groped his crotch saying, "If it works out for you here, then teach Vince all about your kinks, we already know how open he is to learn new things! And Mark and I will always enjoy having sex with the two of you anytime were out here! But if things don't work out, remember, all you have to do is pick up the phone, and I'll come straight out on the bike and collect you! OK?" Paul hugged him again even tighter, his cock miraculously hard again in Steven's firm grasp, despite all the rampant sex he'd had in the barn. Then he climbed back into the car beside Mark, and the two of them set off on their drive home, happy that Paul had found someone of his own, but also just a little sad that he wasn't sitting right there behind them.

Having slept for most of the day, Steven and Mark woke up just after three o'clock in the afternoon. Though fully rested, nevertheless they were both feeling wonderfully lazy, so they lay in each others arms kissing and fondling each other for ages, before Mark threw back the covers and with Steven still lying on his back, Mark got into a 69 on top of him and the two of them enjoyed a slow, loving blow-job in which they both almost worshipped the others rigid cock, as if it were the most precious thing in the entire world to them, keeping up this delirious adoration until neither of them could hold back any longer, and fed his partner with a sweet thick load of hot sperm for breakfast.

After that they climbed off the bed and went into the bathroom, where they enjoyed a leisurely bath together. With their bodies still wet, they came back into their room and worked together to prepare a hot meal and some hot coffee. Then, after washing-up they dressed in T-shirts, jeans and trainers, both of them by then getting used to, and liking the feeling of wearing nothing under their jeans. Just after seven o'clock, Mark carried the sack containing Paul's clothes down to the car, and they set off to drive back to the farm and see how Vince and Paul were getting on together. Feeling happy and completely relaxed, they chatted idly as Mark drove out into the countryside.

As they were going to see Paul and Vince, it was also perfectly natural that most of their conversation was centred around the rampant, horny sex they had all enjoyed in the barn. And they were soon comparing the individual attributes of the sexy, naked bodies of their different sex partners. Also quite naturally, with all the talk about hot and horny sex, their cocks were soon straining inside their jeans, throbbing in their hardness. It was the deliciously painful ache in his cock, that suddenly made Steven remember what Paul had whispered to him, just before they left to drive home.

Laying back in his seat with his legs spread wide, Steven moulded his solid cock with his right hand. Sighing deeply he said, "Paul said something really sweet to me last night, just before we left them!" Glancing across at him Mark replied, "Yeah! What was that then?" Still fondling his cock through his jeans, Steven answered, "As I was hugging him, he whispered in my ear, You and Mark can still give my arse and mouth a good fucking, when you come out to go to the barn you know! I think I'm really going to be happy living out here with Vince. But my body will still be yours, whenever you want it! And I'll make sure and tell Vince that, because without the two of you, Id never have found out what a horny sex-machine I really am!"

Mark grinned broadly and groped his own aching cock. Then he said, "Paul is a really beautiful young bloke, and I hope he and Vince will make a real go of it together! But I hope you also told him that if things don't work out the way he wants them to, he can always come back to us?" Steven at once assured him that he had, and the two of them went back to discussing the individual attributes of all those horny, naked bodies they had enjoyed in the barn. A subject that quite naturally they both really enjoyed, and which continued to keep them feeling as horny as hell, and their cocks painfully hard inside their jeans. Therefore it was little wonder that by the time they parked outside Vince's cottage, they both had only one thing on their minds, having yet more hot and horny action with Vince and Paul.

Walking up the path to the front door, Mark carrying Paul's sack of clothes, Paul opened the door to them wearing only his tatty old jeans, the front of which were fully undone. Instantly he threw his arms around their necks and kissed them both, bubbling with excitement. As he did this, he felt their solid cocks pressing into his thigh and he sighed deeply. Then sliding his hands down over their bodies, he groped the bulging tents in the front of their jeans and smiled wickedly as he said, "Hmmm! Come inside quickly. Vince won't be back for a while yet, but that won't stop me getting rid of these jeans and servicing those two wonderful hard dicks of yours!"

Once inside the cottage, Paul led them into the sitting room, where Mark dropped the sack onto the floor as Paul said, "Thanks for bringing my clothes Mark! That was really good of you." He was already sliding his jeans down his legs, showing his own solid cock standing straight up his stomach as he did so. Then standing naked in front of them, his fingers working eagerly to get them both naked as well, he went on, "Vince is a really horny bastard, just like me!" He laughed, then went on, "And were both a kinky pair of fuckers, and no mistake! Apart from when he took me up to meet the farmer this morning, I haven't had my clothes on once since you dropped us off here last night! And my fucking dicks never had so much attention before!"

He was smiling broadly at them both, and by then he had rid them of their T-shirts, and slid Steven's jeans down his legs to the floor, where having kicked off his trainers, Steven eagerly stepped out of them. Kneeling in front of Steven, Paul immediately opened his mouth, slid Steven's solid shaft inside it and began sucking on it desperately, as he moaned loudly with pleasure. Then after a few seconds, he slid his mouth off it, turned to Mark and quickly undid his jeans and slid them to the floor, taking Marks rampant dick into his hot wet mouth and doing the same. All the time leaving his own throbbing cock untouched, as it bounced around wildly between his smooth young thighs.

After letting Marks aching rod slip from his mouth, he pulled them together so that his hands could caress their firm round arse-cheeks. While at the same time, his warm and eager tongue worked its way all the way up, from one hot young body to the other as he gave them both a toe-curling tongue bath, showing his absolute adoration and devotion to their horny young bodies, running his hands all over their velvet-smooth flesh as he licked and lapped at their already horny bodies and gasped, "But you two will still be able to do anything you want to me! Even though I'm going to live out here with Vince and work on the farm. After all, I owe everything to the two of you, and I really love it when you treat me rough, and show me that I belong to you, and you'll do what you want with me!"

He sighed deeply, just being able to say this to them openly and without any fear, and he wasn't disappointed because Steven and Mark both began running their hands firmly all over his horny young body, making him gasp and sigh as he felt the strength in their hands dominating him. Putting their hands behind his head, pressing his face firmly against their skins as he continued his adoration of them both. Then working his body roughly into position, so that Paul found himself standing, with his legs spread wide and his arms locked around Steven's sexy young body, while Steven held a clump of Paul's hair in one hand, and with the other he wiped his rigid cock all over Paul's face, teasing him with it unmercifully, before he allowed him to slide the throbbing shaft down his hungry cocksucker's throat.

Meanwhile, Mark had spread Paul's arse-cheeks wide, then had also teased Paul by working his cock-head up and down across Paul's desperately twitching fuck-hole, driving their young friend insane with desire. And just at the point when Steven fed his solid shaft into Paul's mouth, so Mark positioned his cock-head against Paul's yearning hole and pushed forward. Quickly he felt his cock slip past Paul's sphincter, so that he was able to feed his throbbing hard shaft all the way up Paul's willing arse while Steven fed his cock into the other end.

Once again Paul was in the position he loved most, his already sweating and horny young body being impaled on two fantastically hard cocks at the same time. He sighed and moaned as he pulled Steven's hips towards himself, burying his cock as deep in his throat as he could get it, knowing the unspeakable ecstasy of realising that those two fabulous dicks were in total control of him, knowing that they could hammer in and out of him, driving him insane with lust, and that he was powerless to stop them; powerless to do anything, except exactly whatever they wanted him to do. And as they both began to fuck his two holes, working their cocks in and out of him, with Mark firmly holding onto his hips, and Steven firmly holding his head in place as their dicks slid into him faster and faster, Paul was ecstatic with joy.

Mark and Steven were still pounding their cocks in and out of Paul's desperately submissive body, when they both heard the front door open, and a few seconds later, Vince walked into the sitting room. He beamed at them both when he saw how they were making use of Paul's eager and horny young body. Without saying a word, Vince quickly stripped out of his own clothes, then came over and kissed first Steven then Mark, then bending forward he kissed Paul in the middle of his sweat-soaked back, running his wet tongue up and down it, making Paul pant and groan even more as his mouth and arse were fucked mercilessly. Then he looked from Mark to Steven and said with a smile, "How about doing that to me now? Paul isn't the only one that likes to get your dicks in both ends at the same time you know!" And he got into the same position as Paul, standing right beside his new lover, spreading his legs wide.

This gave Mark a brilliant idea, and he said to Steven, "Why don't we fuck the pair of them? You know, in and out of one, then in and out of the other!" This sounded like a wild idea to Steven, so they both slid their cocks out of Paul's body at the same time, then Steven fed his cock into Vince's mouth, while Mark lined his cock-head up against Vince's puckered and willing fuck-hole and pressed home, while pressing his hand down on Paul's back, telling him to stay right where he was.

Before long Steven and Mark were having the time of their lives, fucking Vince's two eager holes for a while, then sliding right out of him and spearing Paul's lust-crazed body once again to fuck him for a while, until they were ready to change back to Vince again. In fact they both found this idea so erotic, that each of them shot their hot sperm twice, continuing to fuck through their first orgasms, so that both Paul and Vince got a load of hot sperm deep inside their arses as well as down their throats. And throughout all of this, Vince just like Paul, made no attempt to touch his own rampant aching cock. So that when Steven and Mark finally slipped out of them for the last time, they quickly told the sex-crazed Paul and Vince to get down on the floor in a 69 which they did instantly. And while Steven and Mark collapsed onto the sofa, with their arms around each other, they watched the two desperately horny young lovers attacking each others cocks and bodies with their drooling mouths and hands that roamed everywhere dementedly.

Completely out of their minds with lust, Paul and Vince were sucking and slurping on each others rigid dicks, adoring the objects of their mind-blowing lust and giving Steven and Mark a really horny show of raw, desperate, animal passion, their fuck-holes still gaping wide as the sperm started to ooze out of them. They just couldn't get enough of each other, and nothing on earth could possibly have distracted them from their mutual goal, except perhaps, for another wonderful, hard, throbbing cock!

For over half-an-hour, they devoured each others painfully solid cocks, as well as licking and sucking on each others balls. And when the sight of this proved to be just too much for Steven and Mark and their own cocks swelled again to full aching hardness, they quickly slipped off the sofa back onto the floor again. Working together, they manouvered the two lust-demented lovers' bodies so that Paul was on top. Then Mark easily slid his once more rampant cock right up inside Paul's arse, sighing deeply as he felt it envelope his throbbing shaft, while Steven straddled their friends' bodies, his legs spread wide, and fed his own solid cock deep into Mark's hungry mouth. In only a few seconds, the feel of Mark's rigid dick fucking his arse again tipped Paul over the edge, and he fired off his hot load of spunk deep into Vince's throat.

This in turn triggered Vince to release his hot sperm into Paul's desperately hungry mouth. And while the two of them lay moaning and gasping, Mark again hammered his solid rod in and out of Paul's beautifully fuckable arse, until he felt Steven filling his mouth with hot sweet sperm, which then made him fire off a third load into Paul's eagerly waiting arse- chute. Then they all collapsed in a heap on the floor and lay still as they kissed each other tenderly and rested in the after-glow of their passions.

Much later, they staggered up to the bathroom and cleaned each other up, then still naked, they made some food and sat together in the sitting room eating and talking happily. It was clear to both Steven and Mark, that Vince and Paul were perfectly happy with each other, and Vince told them that the farmer had no objection to Paul living in the cottage with him. Steven said, "Well, it seems like everything has worked out for all of us! I have Mark, and I'm very, very happy! And it's obvious to me, that the two of you are just as happy together as we are!"

Paul beamed at him, then kissed Vince tenderly and looked at Steven as he said, "You can say that again! And it's not just because we have so much horny sex together either! Vince and I just feel so right together it's totally unbelievable!" He laughed, then he went on, "But like I told Vince already, and he's agreed with me, if it hadn't been for the two of you taking me in like you did, and really helping me find out about myself, we would never have met! So don't forget, we may be lovers, but Vince knows that the two of you can come down here anytime you want, and have me naked, to do whatever you want to me! And on top of that, we can all go to the club once a month and have a really hot orgy with all the other sexy guys, if you want to! So I guess you're right Steven, we are all happy, and were all really good friends that care about each other, and not just sex-partners that meet to fuck and then piss-off out of each others lives again till the next time!"

It was very late when Steven and Mark finally climbed back into their clothes. Paul and Vince remained naked naturally, and after their final kisses and hugs, they left the cottage for the drive home. But in a strange way, neither of them felt as if they were leaving anything behind. Of course they were going back to their own room, and in the morning they would get on with their own lives. Similarly, so would Paul and Vince, who would only have a few hours' sleep before they had to start work on the farm.

Yet just like any other family, whose members go off to do different things, each one of them was content in the knowledge, that whenever they wanted to, they could all come together again, to share their love and enjoy their hot and horny sex with each other. And although for each of them, their particular lover was the most important person in the world, they each felt a deep comfort in knowing that two other people cared about them and wanted their happiness, just as much as their lovers did.

Steven had indeed come a long way since meeting the first Paul, who gave him his awakening to the truth that lay deep inside himself. But wherever that Paul was, and whoever he was with, he hoped, with all his heart, that he had, or would find, his own Mark. His own Vince. His own Paul. So that just like him, he would know the real happiness and fulfilment that comes from being loved and completely accepted, for the person you really are, no matter how kinky or how sex-crazed that might be.